"Good morning, Noah."

The chirpy voice could belong to no one else but Sophie. There was something about her upbeat tone that brought to mind rainbows and glitter and cupcakes.

"Morning," he said, not raising his eyes from the stove. No way did he want to look into those expressive eyes when his thoughts were as scrambled as the eggs he had just cooked.

Sophie Miller was rapidly becoming a problem in his uncomplicated world.

"Did you get settled in last night?" she asked. Her voice was infused with so much cheer and a lightness that he desperately needed to hear at the moment.

Unable to stop himself, he swung his gaze up. Her long titian hair hung down gently in loose waves. Even without a stich of makeup, she shimmered. Her green eyes—the color of Irish moss—sparkled.

She wasn't making things easy for him.

Belle Calhoune grew up in a small town in Massachusetts. Married to her college sweetheart, she is raising two lovely daughters in Connecticut. A dog lover, she has one mini poodle and a chocolate Lab. Writing for the Love Inspired line is a dream come true. Working at home in her pajamas is one of the best perks of the job. Belle enjoys summers in Cape Cod, traveling and reading.

Books by Belle Calhoune

Love Inspired

Alaskan Grooms

An Alaskan Wedding
Alaskan Reunion
A Match Made in Alaska
Reunited at Christmas
His Secret Alaskan Heiress

Reunited with the Sheriff
Forever Her Hero
Heart of a Soldier

His Secret
Alaskan Heiress

Belle Calhoune

HARLEQUIN® LOVE INSPIRED®

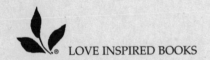

LOVE INSPIRED BOOKS

Recycling programs
for this product may
not exist in your area.

ISBN-13: 978-0-373-21436-5

His Secret Alaskan Heiress

www.Harlequin.com

Printed in U.S.A.

My beloved spake, and said unto me,
Rise up, my fair one and come away with me.
For lo, the winter has past,
the rain is over and gone.
—*Song of Solomon* 2:10–11

For my sister, Patricia, for introducing me
to Daphne du Maurier and Phyllis Whitney.
You started me on the road to romance!

Acknowledgments

For my Love Inspired author friends
who make this profession anything but solitary.
Angel Moore. Alison Stone. Karen Kirst.
Jolene Navarro. Danica Favorite.
Kristen Ethridge. Jessica Keller.
You ladies rock!

For my editor, Emily Rodmell,
for being enthusiastic about this series and
for remembering all the details I tend to forget.

Chapter One

"Here it is. Fresh out of the oven. One reindeer pizza with feta and spinach," Sophie announced in a chirpy voice as she set the order down in the middle of the table. "And a mozzarella salad on the side. It's good for your heart."

"Thanks, Sophie." Jasper Prescott, town mayor, grinned at her, his white whiskers lending him a grandfatherly appearance. She would never admit it to Jasper in a million years, but he was just about the cutest man in the world, despite being an utter rascal. She'd already claimed him as her honorary grandfather. As far as she was concerned, he was a keeper.

"You're quite welcome, Jasper." Sophie smiled at him. "Might I say that ever since you and Hazel got engaged, she's been walking on cloud nine?" Sophie patted him on the shoulder. "Well done!"

Jasper winked at her. "I can't deny that being an engaged man has done me a world of good. I feel as if I have an extra spring in my step." He held his finger up to his mouth in a shushing gesture. "Now don't you tell Hazel I said that. She'll never let me hear the end of it."

Sophie giggled. "I won't say a word, Jasper. It'll be our little secret."

Once the words slipped out of her mouth, Sophie felt a tad guilty. After all, she had been keeping secrets ever since she'd stepped foot into the town of Love, Alaska.

"Now that I'm getting hitched, we need to focus on pairing you up with one of the dozens of men who keep swarming around you.

I've heard lots of gripes from some of them who are part of Operation Love. They're beginning to think you're playing hard to get." Jasper's blue eyes twinkled. "What's wrong, Sophie? None of 'em tickle your fancy?"

Leave it to Jasper to put it all out there with one loaded question. Operation Love was an innovative program he'd created that matched up women from across the United States with rugged bachelors from the small Alaskan fishing village. As town mayor, Jasper had racked his brain to come up with a solution for the shortage of females in town. So far, his program had led to several weddings, more than a dozen engagements and numerous love connections. It was a resounding success.

Jasper's question threw Sophie off balance for a moment. It was the same one she'd been asking herself for more than a year. Why hadn't she been able to move past her ex-fiancé's betrayal and find romance here in town? Despite her fervent prayers for healing, she was still wounded from the past. She had been asked out on more dates than she could count on two hands. And she had never meant to hurt anyone's feelings, but she wasn't going to date a man if the chemistry just wasn't there. And so far, she really hadn't been interested in anyone.

"I want to get hit by that thunderclap, Jasper." She shrugged. "It just hasn't happened yet." She winked at him. "But when it does, you'll be the first to know." What she wasn't telling Jasper was that she wasn't quite ready for romance.

"When you get a free moment, could you bring me an iced coffee?" he asked. "I promise not to bug you about your love life. At least not until tomorrow." The sound of his raspy laughter rang out in the café.

"Sure thing!" She turned in the direction of the kitchen, her eyes landing on a sight that made her stomach do flip-flops. Sophie let out a sigh as she watched her best friend, Grace, sharing a tender kiss with her husband, Sheriff Boone Prescott. They were still newlyweds, having been married last year in a romantic ceremony attended by all the residents of Love, Alaska. Add in one sweet little baby girl named Eva, who was sound asleep in the baby carrier, and it seemed to Sophie that this couple was truly blessed.

She wanted to reach out and shower the newborn with hugs and kisses. Though only a few weeks old, Eva had already won the hearts of the entire hamlet of Love. See-ing Boone and Grace together gave Sophie hope of finding love with a man who would see right down to her soul and the things that mattered most. A man who would love her on her own merits, not just because her father was a billionaire. Not that anyone here in town knew the huge secret she was harboring. As far as they were concerned, she was just plain old Sophie Miller from Saskell, Georgia, a woman who had ven-tured to Alaska to become a part of the Operation Love campaign. The townsfolk had no idea Miller was an alias she was using in order to avoid being connected to the Mattson family name.

Sometimes even Sophie couldn't understand how circumstances had led her straight to this Alaskan hamlet. But all in all, she felt blessed to be here. It was so very different from the world she had left behind in New York City.

Growing up as the only child of coffee magnate Roger Mattson hadn't been easy. Her father—the owner of the Java Giant empire—had raised her all by himself after her parents' divorce and her mother's death a few years later. Although Sophie had been afforded all the luxuries of a royal princess, she'd never had the very things she ached for. A soft place to fall. Her father's undivided attention. People who cared about her for the right reasons. Her entire life she'd been used for her father's connections and the vast fortune everyone assumed she had access to. It had left her feeling jaded and suspicious of everyone's motives. The final straw had been when her father had orchestrated her engagement to his right-hand man, John Sussex. It had all become too much for her—affianced to a man she didn't love and who didn't love her back, with her father pushing her to marry despite her protestations.

And that's how she'd ended up in Love, a remote fishing village in Alaska. Tired of living an unfulfilling life, she'd given up all her credit cards, a penthouse apartment in Manhattan and a hefty bank account. Her father had no idea where she'd gone, and until she could process his staggering betrayal, she intended to lie low. She'd flown to Love simply because she'd seen an article about a women shortage in the town, written by Jasper. Something about the piece had tugged at her heartstrings, and she'd made an impulsive decision to make Love, Alaska, her refuge from the privileged world her father had constructed for her. In the end it had become a gilded cage.

Love, Alaska, on the other hand, was a dream come true. Although she wasn't looking for the man of her dreams at the moment, she still had hope for a happy ending somewhere down the road.

Grace smiled and waved to her from her table. She was the only one who knew her true identity, and Sophie trusted that her best friend would keep her secret, just as she'd promised. Sophie wasn't trying to be deceptive, but she wanted the residents of this quaint village to like and respect her on her own merits, not because of her family's fortune. In her humble opinion, that didn't seem too lofty a goal.

Not to mention the fact that she was currently estranged from her family and had given up all the rights and privileges of being a Mattson.

"Sophie!" Boone beckoned her over with a wave of his hand. Sophie walked to their table, where Eva was now nestled against her mother's chest, Grace soothingly patting her back. "We wanted to ask you something," Boone said, his eyes twinkling.

Sophie clasped her hands together. "Are you going to ask me to babysit this precious little lady? Pretty please with sugar on top."

The couple exchanged a glance, then chuckled. "No, Sophie. We're not quite ready for a date night out without Eva," Grace explained.

"Speak for yourself. I could use a break from diaper changes," Boone teased. Grace shook her head at him and made a tutting sound before swinging her gaze back to Sophie.

Something about her friend's expression seemed sheepish. She ducked her head and focused on Eva rather than looking Sophie in the eye.

"We wanted to ask you if you'd be interested in going out with Dilbert Trask," Boone said. "He's a friend of mine who just moved back to Love. I'm guessing he's been in here a time or two."

"Boone says he's a great guy. And he's been saying some very complimentary things about you," Grace said with a grin.

A hissing sound escaped Sophie's lips. She looked back and forth between her two friends. How could she communicate the fact that she didn't see herself dating Dilbert? "I don't know," she hedged. "Dilbert seems really nice, but I promised myself that I would only go out with a man who made my knees weak."

"Chemistry doesn't always work like that. I didn't swoon when I first met Boone," Grace added.

Boone winked at her. "But you did tumble into my arms."

"I tripped," Grace said, rolling her eyes. "There's a difference."

"So you say," he teased, placing his arm around her and pulling her close. He pressed a kiss against her temple.

Sophie enjoyed the banter between the couple. This was what she wanted for herself. A man who knew her like the back of his hand. An easy camaraderie that always seemed fresh and exciting. Maybe she needed to explore all avenues to find her happily-ever-after. Perhaps Dilbert was the one. How would she know unless she opened herself up to the possibilities?

"Tell you what. Let me think about it. If I keep turning down men who don't give me goose bumps, I'll never find my husband. But on the other hand, I need to have an open mind. My granny always used to say that love is like a spider. It comes creeping out when you least expect it." She grinned at her friends. "I need to get back to the kitchen. We're short staffed these days."

Sophie cast one last lingering look at Grace, Boone and baby Eva. Her heart was filled to overflowing at the joy that bounced off the new family. This time next year, she vowed, she'd have her own man by her side and a clear path to a happy ending. After all, hadn't the whole point of her coming to Love been to become a part of the Operation Love campaign and find her other half?

Noah Catalano parked his rented car on Jarvis Street and swung his gaze around him at the quaint Alaskan village called Love. According to his research, the small fishing village had roughly one thousand residents. Located fifty minutes from Anchorage, Love was situated on the southeastern tip of the state. The town looked like something out of an old-fashioned travel brochure, or a heartwarming postcard. As a native of Homer, he was used to more hustle and bustle than this quaint hamlet. Although Love was picturesque, it would take some getting used to after living in a large city like Seattle for the past five years.

Noah was trying to take it all in. From the looks of it, this town wasn't like anything he was used to. Small shops with brightly colored doors and decorative wreaths beckoned him. So far he hadn't seen many villagers out and about. He couldn't help but grin at the rustic Welcome to Love sign hanging in a store window. Love, Alaska, had a folksy charm most would find hard to resist.

The streets were dusted with snow, courtesy of a January storm that had pummeled a large portion of the state. Even a week later, there was still an abundance of snow on the ground. That was par for the course for Alaskan winters.

Noah took the crumpled photo out of his pocket and smoothed it down on the steering wheel until it was flat. The woman staring back at him was easy on the eyes. With her fiery red hair, the slight freckles scattered across the bridge of her nose and the expressive emerald eyes, she was stunning. No wonder her ex-fiancé was having a hard time letting her go. Maybe his client, John Sussex wasn't crazy, after all, in asking him to keep tabs on his former fiancée.

"You're a beauty, Sophie Miller. I'll give you that," he muttered, before stuffing the photo back inside his coat pocket. "No wonder Sussex can't just let you go."

He let out a low whistle as the full impact of what he'd agreed to do hit him over the head like a sledgehammer. For the next six weeks he was going to be living in this small fishing village in Nowhere's-ville, Alaska, and working a very lucrative gig—keeping tabs on Sophie Miller. He had arrived last night, having been flown in by Declan O'Rourke, a pilot who ran a plane charter business and lived here in town.

As a private investigator, Noah went all over the country following the paying gigs. And he was moments away from beginning his undercover assignment. His company, Catalano Security, had hit a financial rough patch, which had made refusing this job near impossible. And even though he could think of much better assignments than this one, he'd had no choice in the matter. A paying job like this meant that his Seattle-based company might hold on for a little bit longer. He wouldn't have to shutter the doors just yet. And he could pay his employees and allow them to run the fort while he was away. Watching his company go down the tubes wasn't something he could allow to happen.

So, for the foreseeable future, he was going to be posing as a cook for the Moose Café, an establishment owned and operated by Cameron Prescott. It was the same eatery where Sophie worked as a barista and waitress. Noah was going to fulfill his obligation to his client, then head back to Seattle where he belonged, and focus on building up his business.

He knew that he was going to have to be on his A game in order to pull this off. He'd done a little research on Cameron, whose brother, Boone, was the town sheriff. Noah couldn't do anything to raise suspicions about his background. Local law enforcement might run a check on him and hit pay dirt by linking him to his profession as a PI. His company provided personal and corporate security, as well as conducting investigations. It had been rather simple to provide references to his new boss via his connections in the world of private investigations and security. He didn't want to be too cocky about it, since in his experience, that's when people made mistakes.

While in Love, he was going by the name of Noah Callahan. Noah had called in a few favors to make this operation run smoothly. As a result, there was really no reason for anyone to suspect that he was anything other than a man who was seeking to reinvent his life as a cook at the Moose Café. And he had no intention of blowing his cover. His future—and that of his company—was riding on this assignment. Failure wasn't an option.

Sophie waved goodbye to Jasper as he sailed out the door of the Moose Café. Just as he exited, a tall, broad figure stood for a moment in the doorway before crossing over the threshold. Another customer! It was shaping up to be good day for tip money. She loved days like this, when the place was full of hustle and bustle. Interacting with customers was the best part of her job.

The man stood inside the doorway and looked around the premises as if he was soaking in all the details. When he looked up, Sophie sucked in a deep breath.

He was gorgeous, with jet-black hair and striking blue eyes. A dimple on his chin added to the overall wow factor. He had a strong jawline and a commanding air. Although he was on the tall side, it was his leanly muscled physique that really packed a punch. He looked like he could handle himself in a dark alley if needed. He exuded strength.

Sophie let out an involuntary sigh. This man was spectacular. A little piece of Alaskan eye candy.

At the moment he was heading straight toward her, his gait full of power and ease. She wasn't certain, but she might just have to pick her jaw up off the floor. This man was pure poetry in motion. He stopped right in front of her, his gaze focused on her brown apron, which advertised the Moose Café with a cartoon moose sipping a cappuccino. Needless to say, her boss, Cameron Prescott, had a zany sense of humor.

When he swung his head up, Sophie locked gazes with the stranger. "Why, hello there, good-looking." Woops. The words had just slid out of her mouth like a rushing river.

Be quick to listen and slow to speak. Her mother's voice buzzed in her ears. After all these years, Sophie was still trying to learn that lesson. She might benefit from having a zipper on her mouth to prevent this very thing from happening.

She bit her lip, wishing she could take the words back. From the looks of it, tall, dark and handsome didn't seem too impressed by her.

The man raised an eyebrow. His expression displayed a mixture of surprise and a measure of disapproval. Sophie let out a low groan. He appeared slightly humorless. He might have at least cracked a smile at the compliment.

She felt her cheeks blush. "What I meant to say was, hello there, stranger." Why was she fumbling so badly with her words? She didn't want the hottest man in Alaska to think she was a babbling fool. Something told her it might be too late to correct a bad first impression.

"Hello," he said in a deep, calm voice.

She smiled at him, stuffing down her discomfort. "I'm Sophie. Welcome to the Moose Café." She waved her hand in the direction of the seating area. "Feel free to take a seat wherever you like. I'll be right with you with a menu and the most delicious coffee drink you've ever ordered."

He shook his head. "I'm not here to eat," he explained. "My name is Noah. Noah Callahan. I'm here to meet Cameron about the open cook position."

This was the new cook? Marta's replacement? Sophie had completely forgotten that Cameron had said to expect the new hire to show up today. In her wildest imagination she never would have envisioned he would look like this. Sophie had imagined an older, wizened man. The new hire had the appearance of a professional athlete or a fitness model for a sports magazine. Sophie knew it was rude, but she couldn't seem to stop staring at him. In a town full of hot Alaskan bachelors, this guy was perhaps the most gorgeous one she'd laid eyes on yet. And his cornflower blue eyes were magnetic.

"You're the new hire?" she asked, her voice oozing shock and awe.

"Unless you know something I don't," he quipped. "I hope I haven't come all the way to Love for nothing."

"No! No! Of course not. Cameron told me to expect you, but I forgot that you were coming by today. And I wasn't expecting someone so..." Her voice trailed off.

"So what?" he asked, his brows knitted together. His eyes were as piercing as laser beams.

So dreamy. The words popped into her head, although she didn't dare utter them out loud.

"You must be Noah." The sound of Cameron's voice coming from directly behind her caused Sophie to let out a huge sigh of relief. Saved by the boss from any further embarrassment! She wasn't sure exactly how she would have answered Noah's question without humiliating herself even more.

Cameron stepped forward and said, "Cameron Prescott. Nice to meet you." He stuck out his hand and shook Noah's vigorously. "I see you've met Sophie."

"Yes," Noah said with a nod. "Nice to meet you, as well, Cameron. And thanks for letting me rent your place. It saved me the trouble of having to search around town for digs." Noah grinned from ear to ear. Mmm. So the man did know how to smile. And what a nice smile it was. Pretty white teeth and dimples for days. Something told Sophie that Noah Callahan was going to leave the women of Love in quite a flutter, starting with herself.

"No problem at all," Cameron said. "I moved into my wife's home after Paige and I got married, so I'm happy to rent the place out."

Noah was going to be living at Cameron's old place! Sophie let out a little sigh of disappointment. Why hadn't she thought of asking Cameron to rent it to her? Her cabin at the Black Bear Cabins was a tad on the small side. In the past year she had filled up the small space almost to overflowing. Relocating to Cameron's former home would have been amazing. The backyard had a lovely view of the mountains. Oh, well. She didn't believe in crying over spilled milk or lost opportunities.

Gratitude. She had to remind herself that she'd vowed to be thankful for all the things in her life, great and small. She wouldn't dwell on the size of her living quarters or lament the fact that Noah had scooped up Cameron's place. God had already blessed her in so many ways. She wasn't about to grumble.

Living in Love was a world apart from the rarefied atmosphere she'd grown up in. As the daughter of a very wealthy man, there had truly been nothing she couldn't have procured with a single phone call or a word with her father. A private jet. Shopping sprees. Front-row concert tickets. Diamond earrings. The world had been her oyster. Once Java Giant had taken off, her family had relocated to New York City from her small hometown of Saskell, Georgia. They had moved from a modest, ranch-style home to a penthouse in Manhattan.

Sophie wasn't sure she'd ever managed to adjust to being the Java Giant heiress. Most times, she'd yearned to go back to simpler times, when picking peaches and attending church picnics had been the norm for their family. Everything had changed when her father's business took off and went national. Their lives had transformed in an instant. Her upbringing had been lavish, yet it had never brought her true happiness. She'd vowed to strip herself of the luxuries and get down to basics here in Alaska. So although she felt disappointed about Cameron's house, she wasn't going to dwell on it. Material things were fleeting.

"Sophie, can you show Noah around?" Cameron asked, drawing her out of her thoughts. "He'll be starting tomorrow morning, bright and early. I'm going to finish out the cooking shift and show Noah how the kitchen works in a little bit. Hazel will work the tables."

A loud banging sound, following by shouting, emanated from the kitchen. Cameron raised his eyebrows and let out a nervous laugh. "Excuse me. I need to go check in with Hazel. She's a little swamped at the moment. Welcome, Noah. It's great to have you on board."

Sophie smirked, knowing her close friend Hazel Tookes probably wasn't at her best at the moment. As Cameron's honorary mother figure, Hazel was, for all intents and purposes, a silent partner in the café. She allowed Cameron to manage the restaurant and act as the public face of the establishment. Outspoken and lively, Hazel didn't hesitate to let Cameron know when something didn't sit well with her. Working the grill wasn't her forte. Waitressing suited her more, due to her tendency to be a social butterfly.

Noah's gaze trailed after Cameron. Then he looked around the café. "This seems like a popular spot."

"It is. We've been blessed with a loyal following and enough customers to keep this place up and running. Did you know that most businesses fail within the first year?" Sophie couldn't count how many times her father had shared that fact with her. It made her doubly proud of Cameron's success. He'd worked hard for it.

Noah scratched his jaw. "I think I've heard that statistic. It's tough to get a business started, not to mention keeping it profitable."

"That's for sure," Sophie said with a nod. "The Moose Café is a testament to Cameron's hard work and vision. Before I arrived in town, Love endured a recession that caused quite an economic downturn. A lot of businesses didn't make it. But that didn't stop Cameron from stepping out on a limb of faith and opening up this establishment. And the town has rebounded and we have a new factory that mass produces genuine Alaskan boots. They're called Lovely Boots and they've really taken off."

"It's pretty courageous to start up a new

company in the shadow of such hard times," Noah said. "It's a testament to his work ethic and vision."

"No guts, no glory," Sophie proclaimed as she raised her fist in the air, earning another raised eyebrow from Noah.

"Let me show you around," Sophie said, wanting to fill the awkward silence. She motioned for Noah to follow her. She couldn't shake the feeling that he was staring at her as if she was somewhat of an odd duck. His expression was a bit shuttered and he seemed to be quite serious about everything. Maybe he was nervous about the new job. It would be a shame if this hottie was a stick-in-the-mud with a sour disposition.

Life was too short not to smile. Ever since she'd been knee high to a grasshopper, this had been her personal motto. So many people made storm clouds when their lives could be filled with rainbows and glitter and cupcakes.

As Sophie showed Noah around the establishment, she couldn't help but notice that he was a man of few words. Other than some nods and monosyllabic replies, he'd given her nothing but silence. Perhaps he was the strong, silent type—observing everything but giving away nothing. Maybe she just needed to pull him out of his shell.

"How about an espresso or a mochaccino?" she asked, as she led him past the area where they were made.

"No, thanks, Sophie. I'll take a water, though."

"C'mon. Live a little," she teased. "Our coffee drinks are the best thing since sliced bread. Once you taste one of 'em, you won't be able to resist them."

He shook his head. "Thanks, but I'm not really a coffee drinker."

Sophie felt her eyes widen. Not a coffee drinker? And he was going to be working at a popular coffee joint in town? Humph! As the daughter of a coffee magnate, Sophie had a hard time wrapping her head around the notion that Noah didn't like coffee. It was downright peculiar.

He shrugged. "Sorry. I just never took to it."

She didn't know what to make of that statement, but didn't want to hurt the new cook's feelings by poking him about it. Because she'd grown up in the midst of a coffee empire, she found Noah's philosophy rather shocking.

Sophie led him down the hall toward the kitchen. She paused to grab a cold bottle of water from the fridge and handed it to Noah. "No need to apologize. Speaking for myself, I've always loved coffee. When I was little girl I remember waking up to the smell of it." She closed her eyes and breathed in deeply through her nostrils. "Daddy always loved coffee. All types. He would make all these specialty drinks at home right from our kitchen. Mama used to make coffee ice cream for him with one of those old-fashioned ice-cream makers. I used to love when she'd let me turn the handle. I think the love of coffee was imprinted on my DNA."

Sophie blinked back tears. A sudden wave of homesickness washed over her. Despite everything that had transpired between them, she missed Daddy terribly. Home was still etched on her heartstrings. Everything she'd ever learned about coffee had come straight from her father. *There's love in the bottom of every cup.* That was the Java Giant motto. Just thinking about it triggered a feeling of loss so vast it made her heart ache. Even though her father had transformed over the years into a man whose sole focus was his coffee empire, she still loved him and she always would. Ditto for Mama, who was now in heaven. Her parents' divorce had shattered her childhood, but it hadn't made her love them any less. All her memories from her childhood in Georgia were still imprinted on her heart like a permanent tattoo.

Noah seemed to be studying her. "Hey. Are you all right?" His voice was infused with concern. Sky blue eyes radiated compassion.

She sniffed back tears. "I'm fine. Just feeling a little nostalgic today. I love being here in Alaska, but I miss my folks like crazy."

"I'm not surprised to hear that. Family is the most important thing, bar none," he said.

Sophie nodded. "I feel very fortunate to have a family right here in Alaska. Cameron. Hazel, who you'll meet in a few minutes. My best friend, Grace. Jasper, the town mayor. They're not blood related, but they treat me like one of their own. I love them very much." She knew she was gushing, but she couldn't help herself. When it came to Love, Alaska, she tended to wear her heart on her sleeve.

Something resembling understanding flickered in his eyes. He nodded. "That's called community. It's the beauty of a small town. I grew up in one, so I know what I'm talking about. You're very blessed, Sophie." For the first time Noah's voice had a sweetness that warmed her insides. So he wasn't a robot, after all.

Sophie knew she was fortunate to have landed in a heartwarming town like Love just when she'd needed it the most. Her world had crumbled in all around her back in New York City, and she had found a soft place to fall right here in Alaska. For the past year Sophie had been taken under the wing of the townsfolk and treated like gold. In return, she had fallen in love with the small fishing village and its folksy charms.

"I do feel very blessed," she murmured.

For some reason, Noah's words wormed their way inside her and caused her to feel a groundswell of guilt. She had been a resident of this fishing village for more than a year, and for the entire time she had not been forthcoming about her identity or the fact that her father was a billionaire. Although she had tried to convince herself that it didn't matter, she knew deep down inside that withholding the truth from the residents of Love was an act of pure selfishness. In the beginning it had seemed like self-preservation, but with each and every day that passed, Sophie became more and more uncomfortable with the omission. After all, this town had endured near bankruptcy, an embezzlement scandal and severe financial hardships.

Bile rose up in the back of her throat at the mere thought of confessing all to the townsfolk. How in the world would they ever understand her situation? This town had endured business closures, a failed cannery, foreclosures and a severe economic downturn.

No matter how she sliced it, Sophie knew she had to be honest about her family connections before the truth ever came bubbling to the surface. If not, she might risk losing the goodwill and friendship of a whole community of people who trusted her.

Chapter Two

As he headed out of the Moose Café, Noah raised his hand to his chest to steady himself against the feelings rising up inside him. It felt like he'd just run a mile. His heart was beating faster than a drumbeat. It always felt like this when he took on a new assignment. Ever since he'd stepped foot into the Moose Café, pure adrenaline had been racing through his veins.

Noah had ended up working the grill and helping out in the kitchen, finishing the shift alongside Cameron. He'd left right before they locked up the place for the day. He had to admit that cooking at the café hadn't been half bad. It reminded him of working at his family's restaurant, the Highline Diner, in Homer. Before too long he'd fallen into the familiar rhythms of food prep in a kitchen.

He wrinkled his nose. For the life of him he couldn't figure out what had just transpired. Spending time with Sophie and observing her had been his goal, but he wasn't sure he'd been prepared for the experience. Noah hadn't been expecting someone so down-to-earth…and nice.

He shook the feeling off, knowing he was heading into unsafe territory. Once upon a time Noah had seen life through rose-colored glasses when it came to women. Once bitten, twice shy. Life had shown him that he was far too trusting. As a result, he had chosen a career path that involved digging up information to prove without a shadow of a doubt a person's true character. Facts didn't lie. Pictures of husbands stepping out on their wives didn't lie. Money stashed away in secret accounts gave a snapshot of deception.

He was a man who dealt with facts. So far, he knew that Sophie was a woman capable of twisting a man's heart up in knots and abandoning him at his lowest moment. Despite the fact that she was able to plaster on a picture-perfect smile and act as if butter wouldn't melt in her mouth, Noah knew this woman had another side to her.

He needed to get his head out of the clouds and focus. What did it matter if she was nice or nasty? She was a job. Sophie Miller was his target. He didn't want to be friends with her. Didn't want to know her family history. He didn't have any intention of kissing those heart-shaped lips. And he couldn't care less about her adorable Southern twang.

It shouldn't matter to him that Sophie emitted rays as shimmery as the sun and as sugary sweet as an ice-cream sundae. He let out a groan of frustration. He wouldn't be feeling this way if Sophie had been as mean as a snake or bucktoothed and homely.

Don't forget who she is. What kind of woman ditched her fiancé without warning and took off for parts unknown, leaving nothing more than a curt goodbye letter? John Sussex had been emotional and worried out of his mind when Noah had met with him in New York City. Sussex had flown him in to meet with him face-to-face about the assignment.

The way he figured it, there was a sucker born every minute. Sussex had it bad for Sophie Miller. And even though she'd treated him like the gunk underneath her shoe, he still wanted her back. He'd hired Noah to keep tabs on Sophie and to report back to him regarding her romantic attachments. Although he felt a little bit conflicted at first about spying on Sophie, Noah knew his line of work often revolved around surveillance. He wasn't sure why this particular gig left him feeling so out of sorts.

As he got into his car and began driving down Jarvis Street, he looked around at the shops and local scenery. As he passed the Moose Café he spotted the sheriff's office directly across the street, along with a toy store, a barbershop and a trading post. He grinned as he passed a small bookstore called The Bookworm. Tomorrow he might stop in to see if they carried his favorite mystery writer. Suddenly, he noticed a familiar mane of long titian hair with a hot-pink hat perched on top. Sophie! She was bundled up in a winter parka and a pair of sturdy boots. He wondered where she was going, since he'd just heard her say earlier that she was getting a ride home from Hazel.

Given the gloomy-looking sky and a few flakes falling, he hoped that Sophie wasn't venturing too far. *Not my problem*, he reminded himself. Sophie was a big girl, fully capable of making her way around town. So what if it was snowing? Alaska and snow went hand in hand. Sophie was probably used to it by now, even though she was a New York City girl.

He swung his gaze back to the road, then glanced over again at her. The snow seemed to be falling at a faster clip now. He watched as she slipped a little, before managing to catch herself so she didn't fall.

"Atta girl," he said. He wasn't sure why, but he felt like cheering Sophie on. There was something about her that made him want to root for her.

Noah let out a frustrated groan as he watched her continue to trudge onward through the snow. Ever since he was a kid it had been ingrained in him by his father to help out a lady whenever necessary. Chivalry. This time would be no different.

He slowed his car and veered toward the snow-covered sidewalk until he was parallel to Sophie. He pushed the button to let the window down and called out, "Hey, Sophie. Can I give you a ride somewhere?"

She whirled around, her face reflecting

surprise. Then she shifted from one foot to another and rubbed her mittened hands together. "I don't want to put you out, but I'm not sure I can walk all the way to the Black Bear Cabins. It's pretty frosty out here."

He waved her over. "Come on. Hop in."

A cold blast of air assaulted him as soon as Sophie tugged the passenger door open. Her cheeks were rosy as she settled into her seat and put her seat belt on. "You're a lifesaver. I usually get a ride home from Cameron or Hazel, but I think they must have gotten their wires crossed today. I went to get my things, and they'd locked up the place and left."

"No problem. What are the Black Bear Cabins? Sounds like something out of a fairy tale." He couldn't stop thinking about porridge and bears and chairs being broken in a tiny house nestled in the woods. He hadn't been much of a reader as a kid, but he seemed to remember something to that effect.

Sophie chuckled. "Just go straight along this road until you come to the Moose Crossing sign. Once you pass it, you take a right about a half mile down the road and keep going until you see the sign for Black Bear Cabins. That's where I live. I rent out one of the cabins from Hazel, who owns the place. So do a bunch of others who came here for Operation Love."

Noah wrinkled his nose. "Operation Love? That's what brought you here? The matchmaking program?" Noah had heard about it on the Seattle news, and when he'd researched the town of Love it had popped up in the search engine. From what he gathered, it was a program created to pair up single bachelors from here in town with women who came from across the United States. He wondered how successful it had been so far.

Had Sophie found someone? Was she no longer single? Although he suddenly felt tongue-tied, he had to find out if Sophie was romantically attached to anyone here in Love. It was his job to know these things and pass them on to his client.

Something told him John Sussex had no idea that Sophie was part of the matchmaking program. He hadn't mentioned it to Noah when he'd hired him. Had his client been holding out on him? Was there more to Sussex than met the eye? Noah considered himself a pretty good judge of character, but it was possible he'd missed something.

Sophie nodded, her long hair swirling around her shoulders. "Yes. In a way. I came here to reinvent my life, and Operation Love seemed like a good way to find a husband and a loving home."

A husband? Love? Ouch. It wasn't going to be easy relaying that information to Sussex. Noah wanted to shake his head in disbelief, but he didn't want to alienate Sophie, who was giving him the information he needed. Picking her up and taking her to the Black Bear Cabins had yielded more information than he'd imagined.

"You really think your future is here in Love?" There was a tinge of incredulity in his voice that he couldn't manage to mask. He didn't want to sound like a jerk, but he felt amazed that women actually ventured to this town and stepped out in such a massive leap of faith. What if they ended up with a serial killer?

Sophie grinned at him. "The way I figure it, God has always been faithful to me. He placed me here for a reason. I just have to be patient and let it all unfold."

Noah snorted. He hadn't meant to, but it slipped out. One quick glance in Sophie's direction showed that she wasn't pleased in the slightest. Her pretty face was now scrunched up in a massive frown. Her eyebrows were knitted together. He was pretty sure steam might be coming out her ears.

"Excuse me, Noah Callahan, but that was quite rude of you," she huffed. Anger radiated off her in waves.

"I'm sorry, Sophie," he said, feeling contrite. One look into her big green eyes made him feel like the worst person in the world for hurting her feelings. "It just sort of slipped out. Kind of like this morning, when you first saw me and called me good-looking." He winked at her. He wasn't trying to flirt with her, but she was a pretty girl and he liked the way she became easily flustered. That didn't happen too often with the women in his circle. They were all way too polished for his liking.

Noah tried not to grin as he watched Sophie turn several shades of red. She opened her mouth, then closed it, while making a sputtering sound.

"Apology accepted," she finally said. She sat up straight and tilted her chin upward. "I'm sorry if you don't believe that God lights the way for us, but He does. Of that I am very certain."

"It's not that I have anything against the big guy upstairs, but it seems like a pretty tall order to expect Him to give you a happily-ever-after." Noah tapped his brakes as he came to a stop sign. He looked over at Sophie. "Although I admire anyone who believes in something as fervently as you do."

She didn't say a word, but the beginnings of a gorgeous smile began to tug at the corners of her lips. His chest tightened a little bit at the notion that something he'd said had made her smile as if she'd just glimpsed paradise. A wave of happiness traveled through him, and he had to quickly snap himself back to his main objective. He needed information, not million-dollar smiles.

"So, have you found that special someone yet?" he asked, his heart pounding like a jackhammer inside his chest as he awaited her answer. If she said yes, Sussex was bound to be upset.

"No, not yet," she said, her shoulders sagging a little bit. "I've been asked on many a date here in Love, but I've never clicked romantically with any of them. Not that they're not wonderful men, but I'm not willing to settle for anything less than someone who makes me feel like I'm going to swoon. And that hasn't happened yet."

Noah frowned. "Swoon? Isn't that a little bit…unrealistic? I've never heard of a woman actually swooning."

She shook her head at him. "It's a feeling, Noah. One that goes straight down to your toes. Maw Maw used to tell me about it all the time when she talked about meeting Gramps for the first time." Sophie pressed her hands together in a prayer-like fashion. "Her knees felt weak and her belly did flip-flops. She felt light-headed and she actually saw stars."

Maybe she was actually seeing stars in the sky, Noah thought. Far more reasonable than to believe in all the romantic notions Sophie was hurling around.

"Maw Maw?" he asked, curious about the odd-sounding name.

"My granny. Gramps was my granddaddy. The way she described falling in love was like fireworks in July and stars exploding in the heavens. Their love story was one for the ages. No matter what life threw at them, they stuck it out together. Fifty-four years of marriage, bless their hearts." Sophie rubbed her mittens together. "So that's what I want."

"Makes sense," Noah muttered. Humph! About as much sense as women coming all the way to a remote fishing village in Alaska to find single men. He didn't dare say it out loud. No need to alienate Sophie by making any more cracks about Operation Love.

"So, what brought you to Love, Noah? The cook position at the café? Because something tells me it wasn't Operation Love." Sophie's tone was casual, but her expression reflected her curiosity.

"Pretty much. I needed the money," he said. He felt bad about stretching the truth, but he couldn't very well tell her the real reason he was in town. *No, Sophie. I was actually hired by your ex-fiancé to keep tabs on you. It seems he hasn't quite let go of the*

relationship and he paid me an unbelievable
sum of money for the gig.

"Times have been a little rough," Noah
admitted. It was the truth, even if he'd omit-
ted a few parts of the story. Being here in
Love was a surefire way to save his company from going belly-up. If nothing else,
Sussex was paying him well to keep tabs
on Sophie. There was no reason to feel this
twinge of guilt, he reasoned with himself.
He didn't owe her anything.

"I'm sorry to hear that," Sophie murmured, her eyes mirroring her words. "But
Love is definitely the right place to turn
things around. Are you new to Alaska?"

"I was born and raised here in Alaska, so
it's home for me, although living in such
a small town will be something of a new
experience." It would definitely take some
getting used to after being based in Seattle
for the last five years. He wasn't sure where
the market was or the gas station or where
to go to buy a pair of jeans. By the time he

figured it all out it would be time to head back home.

"You'll love it," Sophie said. "I'm from Georgia originally, but my family relocated to New York City. Alaska has been like nothing I've ever experienced before."

Sophie was a Georgia peach! He knew he'd detected a sweet Southern twang. Sussex had forgotten to add that detail in the information he'd provided, which seemed a little odd to Noah.

She jutted her chin straight ahead. "Keep on this road for another mile or so."

Noah let out a low whistle. "This would have been a mighty far way for you to walk."

"I truly appreciate the ride." She let out a giggle. "And so do my feet. You came along at just the right time." Sophie looked around the interior of the car. "Is this yours or a rental?"

"It's a loaner from Hank Jeffries. I figured having wheels would be important in order to make it to work and back home every day."

"Hank is a great guy. He's a firefighter. And he sure loves cars. He has about half a dozen or so."

"Wow. That sounds like quite a collection. What about you? Do you own a car?" Noah asked.

Sophie let out a sigh. "I don't drive, Noah, so a car wouldn't do me much good."

He turned toward her, noticing the sheepish expression plastered on her face.

"You don't have a license?" He tried to keep his voice neutral, but could hear the surprise ringing out in his tone. It was a little unusual not to have your license at twenty-seven.

"No," she said in a small voice. "I never got mine."

"I thought Georgia was one of those states where teenagers got their licenses early. Sort of a rite of passage."

"That's true, but my family moved to New

York City when I was a kid. In a big city getting your license isn't the same as when you're living elsewhere. Taxis. The subway. Buses. There are so many ways to get to where you need to be." She shrugged. "At least that's how it was for me. I would love to learn to drive, though," she said in a wistful voice. "Someday."

"You never know. Someday could be right around the corner," Noah said, surprising himself by his desire to want to soothe her. There had been something in her voice that alerted him to the fact that she wanted to drive way more than she was letting on. He didn't blame her in the slightest. It represented the freedom to go where you wanted when the urge struck you. Even though driving in Alaska in the winter was tricky, it would open up a whole new world for Sophie. Once she was behind the wheel she'd never long for her nondriving days, he imagined.

For the next few minutes they sat in companionable silence, until a rusted-out, faded sign announced that they had reached the Black Bear Cabins.

"Make the turn here," Sophie announced.

Noah turned down a tree-lined, snow-covered road. Stunning white-capped mountains loomed in the distance. Noah knew he had never seen anything quite as spectacular. Not even in Homer. Having grown up in Alaska, Noah knew that his home state was full of stunning vistas. The view from here was a little slice of heaven. He almost wanted to put the car in Park and just sit back and enjoy the landscape for a few minutes.

Dozens of reddish-brown cabins came into view. They exuded a rustic, no-frills air. They reminded him a bit of summer camp at Lake Chilkat when he was ten years old. Noah felt a smile tugging at his lips at the memory of all the good times he'd enjoyed there. He had snagged his first kiss from Penny Adams while they had been enjoying a canoe ride on the lake. By the end of the summer she'd fallen for Jory Banneker and broken Noah's heart.

Sophie navigated the way to her cabin while pointing out where each of her friends lived along the route. Noah didn't even try to keep all the names and facts straight. It wasn't important to his investigation, so he wasn't going to sweat it.

"This is my place right here," she finally announced. A bright red birdhouse hung from the rafters of her cabin. A matching Adirondack chair, dusted with snow, sat on the porch. It looked festive and cheery, much like Sophie herself.

"Would you like to come in for some hot cocoa?" she asked. "It's the least I could do after you rescued me from foot blisters."

Hot cocoa. It had always been his favorite, ever since childhood. He could almost taste it going down his throat with its sweet, rich flavor.

All of sudden, Noah felt the pressure of a

huge weight on his chest. At this moment, more than anything in the world, he wanted to accept Sophie's offer of hot chocolate. But he knew he couldn't. He shouldn't.

Sophie was business. He had been hired to watch her every move. They couldn't be friends, not really. The past had taught him that mixing business with his personal life was a fool's game. He had crossed that line once before and lived to regret it. Noah liked to think that he'd learned from his mistakes. And even though there was something about Sophie that called to him, he was going to do his very best to ignore it.

She couldn't be this nice or this chipper. Buying into her goody-goody act was a fool's game. And he was nobody's fool.

Rather than sip hot cocoa with her, Noah would go to his rental home and call Sussex with his first report on Sophie. He would be impartial and unbiased in reporting the facts to his client. Noah would be professional. He wouldn't talk about how pretty Sophie looked or the way she was acting totally different than the woman Sussex had known who hailed from big cities.

"I'll even throw in some marshmallows," Sophie said in a singsong voice.

He let out a low groan. Marshmallows were his favorite! Especially the miniature ones that were perfect for hot chocolate.

"It's a sweet offer, but I really should head back to the house. I still have some unpacking to do." He had to practically force the words out of his mouth. All he wanted to do was jump out of the car and join her.

"I understand," Sophie said with a bob of her head. "Your new life in Love is waiting to unfold." With a wave of her hand, she added, "Thanks again for the ride. See you tomorrow at the Moose."

Noah watched for a moment as Sophie mounted the steps, pulled out her keys and unlocked the door to her cabin.

He knew that he was in trouble the moment he began praying she would turn around so he could get another glimpse of her. When she did—flashing a smile and another wave of her hand—he felt a little hitch in the region of his heart.

Pressing his foot way too hard on the gas, Noah roared away from Sophie, the promise of hot cocoa and the Black Bear Cabins. During the entire ride back to town Noah berated himself. He had been here less than twenty-four hours and somehow Miss Sophie Miller had managed to make him forget for a short period of time that she was his assignment.

He vowed to do better. Tomorrow was another day to get things right. And not for a single second did he plan to take his eyes off the prize. This assignment was crucial to the future of Catalano Security. He couldn't mess up this golden opportunity.

Noah gripped the steering wheel tightly. Sophie couldn't be his friend. He shouldn't even allow himself to acknowledge she was attractive. He couldn't accept invitations for hot chocolate. He wouldn't let himself cross certain lines with her. He'd done that once before, and in the process, turned his entire life upside down. Fool me once, he reminded himself. He'd learned a few hard lessons over the past few years. He wasn't going to get dazzled by a client. Not again.

Sophie Miller wasn't going to make a fool out of him.

Chapter Three

The next morning Noah made it to the Moose Café by six thirty. He actually beat Cameron there and greeted him as he arrived to open up the place.

"Now that's what I like to see," Cameron said with a wide grin. "Another early bird like myself. We probably won't see Hazel or Sophie until at least seven."

Noah almost sputtered at the "early bird" comment. It had taken every ounce of discipline he had to get his weary body out of bed this morning. And it hadn't been easy. From the moment Noah rose at the crack of dawn, he had felt like a grizzly bear with a sore paw. Years of working late-night stakeouts as a PI and sleeping in the next morning had taken their toll on him. He was definitely not an early bird.

After tossing and turning for hours last night, he had finally realized that Sophie must be a chameleon. She had the ability to change her personality at the drop of a dime depending on the circumstances. Humph! He had come up against women like her before. Charming and manipulative. And he wasn't about to fall for her sweetness-and-light routine. If she was that genuine she wouldn't have dumped her fiancé and headed to Alaska to find a new man, without batting an eyelash.

And Noah had a sneaking suspicion that there was more to her being here in Love than met the eye.

Last night he had called Sussex shortly after dinnertime. The conversation had been awkward and sad, as well as eye-opening.

Noah had given Sussex a rundown of his interactions with Sophie, starting off with her admission about being part of the Operation Love program. He knew that hearing this kind of news would feel like a kick in the gut, especially since Sussex appeared to be head over heels in love with Sophie.

Sussex had let out a shocked gasp upon hearing the news. "She's part of a matchmaking program? No! That can't be right."

"Yes, it's true. I heard it straight from her own lips," he'd acknowledged. "Sorry to have to tell you that kind of information, but I have to stick to the facts."

A tortured silence ensued, during which Noah was certain he heard slight sniffling sounds on the other end of the line. The poor guy was a puddle of mush. Meanwhile, Sophie seemed upbeat and content with her life in Love. Their situations were night and day.

He might as well throw the guy a bone. "She's still single and unattached, though, if it's any consolation," Noah added.

"Yes, it is," Sussex had replied, his tone sounding more upbeat. He cleared his throat. "It gives me hope."

Noah's heart had gone out to him. He was clearly besotted with Sophie, the woman who had run out on him. And judging by her desire to find a loving home in Alaska, she didn't seem to be losing any sleep over her ex-fiancé. That bugged Noah. It showed a coldness in Sophie's personality that didn't speak well of her. A woman who tossed men aside like garbage wasn't to be trusted or admired. He didn't care one bit how likable she seemed. He knew all too well that some women found it easy to play a role.

The whole thing rankled him more than he cared to admit. He knew what it felt like to be ditched. Abandoned. And he hated the fact that Sophie had twisted this man around until he hadn't known if he was coming or going. Although he had wanted to tell Sussex to get a grip on his feelings and move on, Noah knew that rich men didn't listen to peons like himself. No, it had been apparent from Sussex's expensive suits, fancy car and the fact that he'd paid in cash that he was a considerably wealthy man.

And what was that saying people always quoted? "The heart wants what it wants." John Sussex wanted Sophie back something fierce. But just because he wanted her back didn't mean it was going to work out that way. Sophie seemed to have moved on.

Noah didn't know what Sussex's end game was with regards to Sophie. Was he waiting for her to fall for someone, then swoop in to try to win her back? Did he love her so much that he just needed to make sure she was safe and sound? Or was he testing the waters so he could develop a strategy? It was a head-scratcher.

Noah's instincts were now on high alert. He still felt as if there was something his client wasn't telling him. Had he been so eager for the big payout that he'd missed a few red flags?

He set a pan down on the stove with a slight bang. Why was he fretting so much about this assignment? He couldn't allow himself to get emotionally involved. Sure, Sophie had made a great first impression on him, but he suspected it was all smoke and mirrors. She had been way too much of a sweetheart. In other words, too good to be true. In his experience, people weren't that good-hearted.

Do the job, then take the money and run! It was the smartest way to handle things, considering what he stood to lose if this assignment went off the rails. Just the thought of having to shutter the doors of his company made him feel sick inside. It was the only thing in this world he had ever built for himself out of his own ingenuity and savvy. He couldn't lose it! And getting tied up in knots about Sussex's agenda and the inconsistences about Sophie could only muddy the waters.

"Good morning, Noah." The chirpy voice

could belong to no one else but her. There was something about her upbeat tone that brought to mind rainbows and sunshine and puppy dogs.

"Morning," he said, not raising his eyes from the stove to meet her gaze. No way did he want to look into those expressive eyes when his thoughts were as scrambled as the eggs he had just cooked for Cameron.

Sophie's image had danced under his eyelids last night as he'd tossed and turned. If he didn't get it together, things were going to get mighty complicated rather quickly. And Noah didn't like complicated. He liked orderly and straightforward. He hated curveballs. Sophie Miller was rapidly becoming a problem in his uncomplicated world.

"Did you get settled in last night?" she asked. Her voice was infused with so much cheer and a lightness he desperately needed to hear at the moment.

Unable to stop himself, he swung his gaze up. Even in the dullest of brown shirts, Sophie looked resplendent. Her long titian hair hung down in loose waves. Without a trace of makeup on her face she still shimmered. Her full lips were a perfect shade of pink. Her green eyes—the color of Irish moss—sparkled. She had a pleasant expression on her face, one that caused a slight uptick in the beating of his heart.

He frowned. She wasn't making things easy for him. Another wave of sympathy for Sussex roared through him.

"Pretty much," he said curtly. He didn't want to encourage too much conversation with her, at least not until he could get a handle on how best to deal with her. Noah needed to figure out how to get close to Sophie without things becoming too personal. There needed to be an invisible line drawn in the sand, one he couldn't step across. Establishing boundaries was a good idea.

"How are you liking Cameron's place?" Sophie asked. "I always thought it had such fantastic views of the bay. At night you can really catch a glimpse of the constellations."

"It's nice," he said, reaching up for an order slip. He pretended to study it so he wouldn't have to look in Sophie's direction again.

"And it's fairly close to everything in town, so it will be really convenient for you. Not to mention you don't have much of a commute to work," she continued. "That will be a lifesaver when it's storming outside or the roads are icy. Or even if you want to pick up something at the post office."

"I imagine so," he muttered. Although he sensed Sophie meant well, her friendly demeanor was making his assignment exponentially more cumbersome.

She continued to chatter away. "Just wait till you meet Emma, Cameron's little girl. She's a charmer if there ever was one. And Cameron's wife, Paige, is wonderful." Sophie shook her head and her mane of red hair rippled across her shoulders. "Matter of fact, everyone here in Love is pretty amazing. You'll see what I'm talking about once you start meeting folks."

"I'm kind of busy here, Sophie," he snapped.

He instantly saw the hurt flash in her eyes. She resembled a wounded deer. A piercing sensation stabbed him in the gut. He hadn't meant to sound so harsh, but pushing her away had felt like throwing himself a life preserver. It was difficult to establish boundaries between them when Sophie was treating him like her new best friend.

It took her a moment to recover. "Okay, then," she said in a crisp tone. "I won't waste another second of your time." She turned on her heel and disappeared from the kitchen as if her feet were on fire.

Once she'd gone, Noah let out a tortured groan. He wanted to follow after her and apologize, but he knew the words would just stick in his throat. He'd never been good at smoothing things over.

Well, he'd just managed to solve his problem regarding Sophie's close proximity to him. He had just proved to her without a shadow of a doubt that he was a total jerk. Noah couldn't imagine that she'd want anything further to do with him. And that thought left him feeling way more shattered than he could have ever imagined.

Sophie blinked away the tears that had pooled in her eyes. She wasn't sure whether she was furious or embarrassed. Who did Noah Callahan think he was, anyway? He was a newbie in town, and since she had been in that position herself, she'd wanted to show him grace and kindness and fellowship. Everyone in Love had treated her with compassion when she had arrived here. She had just been trying to pay it forward with Noah!

Clearly, that had been a major mistake.

Noah had been all kinds of wonderful yesterday when he'd rescued her from a long walk to the Black Bear Cabins. What had happened to alter his mood so drastically? Sophie thought he'd been as sweet as peaches and cream yesterday. She'd been looking forward to getting to know him better. Last night she'd thought of him before she closed her eyes to go to sleep. He had been so kind, and she respected the way he had come to Love for a steady job and a regular paycheck. That took gumption!

Of course, the fact that he was very easy on the eyes didn't hurt. A sigh slipped past her lips. His looks were scrumptious. She couldn't deny it. There was something about Noah that she found very appealing.

Not that his good looks mattered at the moment. There was nothing more of a turn-off than a cutting tongue and incivility. Rudeness was not attractive! It totally went against Sophie's philosophy about greeting the world with a warm smile and encouraging words. Every single day she put her best foot forward and stepped out on a limb of faith. It was her goal to treat people with kindness. Maybe he was one of those men who knew he was good-looking and tended to act as if he was God's gift to the universe.

Humph. It would be a hot winter's day in Alaska before she put herself out there again with Noah Callahan! Perhaps the ladies in his life put up with his snotty ways, but she wasn't about to put up with his churlishness.

With her head held high, she moved toward the table where her next customer sat awaiting service. "Morning, Dwight. Can I start you off with some coffee before I take your order?"

"Why hello, Sophie." Dwight Lewis clutched the menu in his hand and peered past her, adjusting his glasses as if he might be able to see better in doing so. Dressed in his signature suit and bow tie, he made Sophie wonder if he ever dressed down in jeans or a sweater. A smile tugged at her lips at the thought of a dressed-down Dwight. She might not even recognize him.

"Are you waiting for someone to join you?" she asked, saying a silent prayer that he was meeting up with someone special for an early-morning date.

Dwight Lewis was the town treasurer. Although Sophie knew that he meant well, he tended to rub people the wrong way with his desire to keep the books balanced in a town that had almost gone belly-up financially a few years ago. He had a tendency to act like a know-it-all.

Sophie had a feeling that Dwight was just lonely. He had tried on several occasions to pair up with women from the Operation Love program, but so far nothing had stuck. Bless his heart. He deserved love just as much as anyone else in this lovelorn town.

"I, um... Marta usually pops in to say hello when I come for breakfast. Is she around? I haven't seen her for a few days." Dwight's gaze darted about the restaurant as he spoke.

Marta! Sophie had totally forgotten that she and Dwight had gone out on a few dates.

Hadn't Marta told him about her plans? Sympathy flared inside Sophie at the realization that Dwight was about to get his feelings hurt.

She reached out and patted his shoulder. "Oh, Dwight. I'm sorry to be the one to tell you, but Marta had to go back home for an emergency. She gave notice to Cameron a few weeks ago about having to give up the cook position."

Dwight resembled a startled owl as he looked up at her. "What? When did she leave?"

Sophie thought for a moment. "Almost a week ago."

Dwight's Adam's apple bobbed as he swallowed. "W-when is she supposed to return?"

"I—I'm not sure she's coming back, Dwight," Sophie said, her heart aching as the man's face fell. He appeared stunned by the news. Although Marta was a nice, unassuming woman, Sophie could wring her neck right now for wounding Dwight like this. Despite his brash attitude, he was a gentle soul.

He bowed his head for a moment, then placed the menu facedown on the table and slowly stood up. "I think I'll forgo breakfast this morning. I don't have much of an appetite, after all." He briskly walked past her, his gaze focused on the exit.

"Wait, Dwight," she called after him. "If you'd like a listening ear, we could talk over coffee."

Sophie watched as he slinked out of the café without bothering to answer her. His heart had shattered right before her very eyes. It sent a chill straight through her. If this was love, did she really want to have anything to do with it?

"What was that all about?" Hazel asked in a booming voice as she came up behind Sophie. With her tall height and commanding air, the woman could be a bit intimidating. She was a straight shooter who didn't mince words. But in Sophie's eyes, her friend was a real sweetheart and all-around mother figure.

Sophie shrugged. "He was looking for Marta. If I had to hazard a guess, I think he's in love with her. And now he's heartbroken because she's gone and she didn't even have the courtesy to tell him she was leaving Love."

Once again this morning, Sophie found herself blinking away tears.

Hazel patted her on the back in a soothing gesture. "Now, now, don't fret about it. We can't judge Marta because we really don't know the entire circumstances. Things will work out for Dwight, one way or another." Hazel shook her head. "He's the most exasperating man I've ever met, but I still want him to find his happy ending." She wagged her eyebrows at Sophie. "I'm praying for you to meet your match, as well. Every night before I go to bed I kneel down and ask God to show you favor, Sophie."

Tears slid down her cheeks. Knowing

Hazel prayed for her was incredibly moving for Sophie. "Thank you, Hazel. For everything. You've given me roots here in Love. That's priceless."

"Everyone needs to be firmly planted somewhere. Now, I haven't pried into your past, and it hasn't escaped my attention that you haven't been very forthcoming about it." When Sophie opened her mouth, Hazel hushed her. "I'm not complaining, but I would like to point out that perhaps you need to get past whatever is holding you back from finding that man of yours. It's fine to say you're part of Operation Love, but remember the love part."

"I want to find love," Sophie acknowledged. "And maybe my past is hindering me from doing so," she hedged. "But I really want things to change for the better in the romance department. If I have to face up to my truths to do it, then so be it."

Hazel sent her an exaggerated wink. "Well, why don't you go flirt with our handsome new employee while I go make some coffee drinks? These orders need to go up." Hazel handed Sophie some order slips and made a shooing motion in the direction of the kitchen.

Sophie didn't bother to make a fuss. At some point or other she would have to interact with Noah again. There was no sense in telling Hazel or Cameron that the new hire had made her feel awful earlier. Knowing Cameron, he would take Noah to task for it. He was as protective of her as an older brother. And Hazel was such a firecracker. There was no telling how she would react. No, it was best to keep quiet and handle the situation with grace and dignity.

Sophie made her way to the kitchen and placed the two order slips on the spindle. It would be Noah's job to take the slips down and prep the food. She didn't even have to look at him if she didn't want to. His back was to her and he was cooking something that smelled scrumptious.

There weren't any dishes at the pass-through, but a plate sat on the butcher-block table directly behind Noah. Not wanting to speak to him, Sophie reached out for the plate, then instantly recoiled as heat seared her palm and fingers. The plate clattered to the floor. She let out a cry and closed her eyes as pain seared her hand.

"Sophie. Are you all right?" She watched through a red haze as Noah whirled around and reached her side in seconds. "Is it your hand?"

She nodded, gritting her teeth at the agony caused by the burn. He gently reached for her wrist and examined the damage.

He let out a tutting sound. "It looks like a third-degree burn. You need some salve for it and a bandage." Noah's eyes were intense as he locked gazes with her. She nodded solemnly. All of a sudden she knew that she was in great hands. Noah was confident and masterful. He was taking charge of the situation.

"Where's your first-aid kit?" he asked.

She jutted her chin in the direction of the sink. "In the top drawer."

Noah turned around and headed toward the drawer. He pulled it open, yanking out the kit and rummaging around until he found ointment and a large Band-Aid.

"Sit on the stool," he commanded, nodding toward it. Sophie sat down and peered up at him as he bent over and began patching her up. His movements were gentle and precise as he placed the ointment on her hand and wound a white cloth bandage around it. "The burn is in an awkward place, particularly for a server. It's going to be tender for a bit and you're going to have to put ointment on it regularly so it doesn't get infected."

"Thanks, Noah. It was stupid of me to reach for the plate without asking about it. If it had been ready to be served you would have put it at the pass." It had been foolish to just pick up the plate, but she'd been so annoyed with Noah that she hadn't wanted to communicate with him. She'd been childish. The burn had been the result of her pride.

"We need to communicate better, since we'll be working together." He patted his hand against his chest. "I don't blame you for not wanting to talk to me. I'm so sorry about earlier. I acted like a jerk. I hope you won't hold it against me." His eyes were filled with contrition. In one instant, Noah wore down her defenses. How in the world could she hold a grudge against a man who had bandaged her up so nicely?

"Got up on the wrong side of the bed this morning?" she teased.

"I'm not exactly a morning person," he admitted. "I don't function well unless I get my eight hours."

"Well, here's a little tip that I learned when I first arrived in town. At night, crack your window just a wee bit so you can get a dose of pure Alaskan air. If that doesn't give you a perfect night's rest, I don't know what will."

"I'll take that advice, Sophie," Noah said.

"I better get back at it before the customers start a revolt. Gimme a few minutes for the eggs, sausage and pancake order." After flashing a perfect smile, Noah turned back toward the stove and began cooking up a storm. Sophie stood and watched him for a few moments, admiring his strong arms and the powerful slope of his neck. Knowing she might be ogling him, she forced herself to leave the kitchen and head back to the dining area.

She felt as light as a feather. A sense of euphoria rose up inside her. Sophie felt as if she was floating on air.

All this time she had been hoping and praying to meet a man who gave her goose bumps. And now, out of the clear blue sky, it had happened. Kismet. A connection. The entire time Noah had been nursing her wound Sophie had been trying to figure out the sensations coursing through her.

Goose bumps! The same type Maw Maw had always told her about. And it came from an unlikely person. Despite the fact that he'd been an absolute jerk, Noah Callahan had given her goose bumps. Finally, after all these weeks and months, an Alaskan hottie had made her feel something worth rejoicing over. A real honest-to-goodness romantic connection. There was no doubt about it as far as she was concerned. For the first time in well over a year, she felt an earth-shaking, heart-pounding attraction to a man.

All of a sudden, she felt her enthusiasm come to a crashing halt. Hazel's heartfelt words had forced her to realize that she had been reluctant to find love because of the lie she'd been living. And nothing had changed in that regard. She was still harboring secrets about her true identity and economic status.

Noah was a man who had come to Love in need of a job and a steady paycheck. Guilt threatened to choke her. She had never been in his precarious position. Even now she had a safety net—her father and a trust fund set up in her name. Noah was clearly just getting by in life and trying to put one foot in front of the other in order to keep himself solvent. It would be the height of irony if she became involved with a man who seemed to be struggling to make ends meet.

An uncomfortable feeling settled in Sophie's chest. For a moment she found it a little hard to breathe. For so long she'd wondered why none of the men in Love had appealed to her on a romantic level, despite all their wonderful attributes. The truth was staring her straight in the face. Most of the men in Love held blue-collar jobs, and due to the town's recession a few years ago, were working hard to stay financially afloat. A part of her had felt too guilty about her wealthy origins to fully commit to looking for a partner.

There was no getting around it. The fact that she was a billionaire's daughter masquerading as a barista-waitress might not sit well with an average Joe like Noah. He was a working-class man who might not understand why an heiress was masquerading in an Alaskan fishing village as a waitress.

Dear Lord, please help me figure a way out of this mess. For the first time in what seems like forever, I feel a few stirrings in my heart. Noah intrigues me. But I've been living with this lie for so long that I'm frightened of what might happen if I tell the truth. I've built a life for myself here in Love and my friends have become like family. I don't want to lose them. Please shine a light for me so I can find my way toward the truth.

Chapter Four

Noah whistled an upbeat tune as he readied himself for his shift at the Moose Café. Strangely enough, he was getting used to morning hours. He'd made it a daily ritual to go outside to Cameron's back porch and watch the sun rise as it crept up over the mountains. This view was food for his soul. He inhaled a deep breath of pristine Alaskan air, then slowly exhaled. Noah had the strangest sense that he was exactly where God wanted him to be at this very moment in time.

Being here in Love reminded him so

much of his upbringing in Homer. Sometimes Noah forgot all the wonderful things that made Alaska so magnificent. He now wondered if he'd deliberately suppressed those memories so he wouldn't miss home so much. He had always been of the belief that the only way he could make his mark in the world was to leave the place he had always called home. Alaska.

But now he was beginning to wonder about that decision. Had he made things way more complicated than they'd needed to be? Could he have built up a successful security business right here in Alaska on his home turf? It was a complex question, one he needed to delve into at another time.

For now, he simply stood in humble awe and appreciation of the raw beauty of this land he loved so much. His gaze focused on the craggy mountains looming in the distance. The glistening waters of Kachemak Bay stretched out for miles and miles, as far as the eye could see. The wintry climate invigorated him. A feeling of gratitude swept over him, as strong and sure as he was standing here.

Lord, I know I haven't called on You in a very long time, but thank You for creating this rugged land, this place of unsurpassed grandeur. Thank You for reminding me of the beautiful masterpiece You created and for bringing me back to this place that's so much a part of who I am.

By the time Noah arrived at the Moose Café, the restaurant was already lit with a warm, golden glow. Although the Closed sign was still up, the front door was unlocked, and as he walked in the tinkling of the bell heralded his arrival. He greeted Cameron and Hazel, who were sitting at a table drinking coffee and eating a few of the doughnuts he'd whipped up yesterday.

"Morning, Noah!" Hazel greeted him. She waved him over to the table. "Come on and sit with us for a spell. We don't open up this joint for another twenty minutes, so we're enjoying some downtime before the deluge begins."

Noah always found himself grinning whenever Hazel spoke to him. She was a lively and warm woman who didn't hesitate to speak in blunt terms. He liked her spunk.

"So, Noah," she drawled. "I've been meaning to ask you something."

"Uh-oh," Cameron said, reaching for his coffee cup and taking a lengthy swig from it.

"Ask away," Noah said, instantly regretting his openness once Cameron began sending signals with his eyes.

"Are you single?" Hazel asked without skipping a beat.

He felt a smile twitching his lips. "Yes, I'm single."

"That's a blessing for the ladies of Love, although you're now providing the men here with some stiff competition in the looks department." Hazel's gaze swept over him like laser beams. "From what I've heard through the town grapevine, you're not a participant in Operation Love. Is that true?"

Noah gulped. "I'm part of the town grapevine? I've barely been in town a week."

Cameron let out a loud chuckle. "From the moment you stepped out of Declan's seaplane you became part of it," he explained, quirking his mouth. "That's how small towns work, especially this one."

Noah shook his head in disbelief. He needed to keep low to the ground and not attract any attention to himself. There wasn't time for any distractions, particularly not of the female variety.

"No, I'm not part of Operation Love," he answered.

Hazel leaned across the table and splayed her hands in front of her. "I'm going to be brutally honest, Noah. You're seriously missing the boat by not joining up. Don't you want a happily-ever-after like Cameron and Paige?"

"Technically, I was never part of Operation Love," Cameron interjected. "Paige and I reunited after a few years apart, so we can't really be counted as a success story for the program."

Hazel scowled at him. Cameron shrugged. She turned toward Noah and continued making her pitch. "The women in this program are extraordinary. Imagine the bravery and pluck it took to come all this way in the hopes of finding your one true love? As far as I'm concerned, that type of gal is a keeper."

"I agree," Noah said with a nod. "I have the utmost respect for anyone who takes a huge leap of faith." The last thing he wanted to do was make Hazel think he was looking down on Operation Love. And he couldn't very well tell her that he wouldn't be in town long enough to find a life partner. That would pretty much blow his cover.

The grin Hazel bestowed on him was dazzling. It made him a little nervous. She was acting as if he'd given Operation Love a huge thumbs-up. Perhaps he needed to reiterate that he wasn't interested in the town's matchmaking program.

Just then the bell chimed and they all turned toward the door. Sophie stood there in a puffy down jacket the same color as her eyes. A white beret sat perched atop her head. Her cheeks were rosy. The tip of her nose looked like a raspberry.

"Morning, everyone. It sure is cold out there," she said, rubbing her mittened hands together. "Sorry I'm late, but I stopped in to see Liam at the clinic. Claire gave me a ride into town."

"You're not late," Hazel said. "We still have another ten minutes before the doors open. Take off your coat and sit for a while."

"A hot, steaming coffee would be a nice pick-me-up," Sophie agreed, shrugging off her coat and draping it over one of the chairs.

"Hot coffee coming right up." Hazel jumped up from her seat and made her way to the counter.

Noah's ears perked up. Who was this Liam person? And what was he to Sophie?

Was he a love interest? If so, Noah needed to find out everything he possibly could about this man. It would all be part and parcel of his investigation. He felt a little niggling sensation in his chest. For some inexplicable reason, he didn't want this Liam character to be romantically involved with Sophie.

"So what's my brother up to? Was he able to give you the medicine you needed for your allergies?" Cameron asked, taking another hearty swig from his cup.

"Dr. Liam Prescott is my hero at the moment. He switched up my medicine and gave me a new inhaler. Hopefully now I can breathe at night," Sophie said. "And Ruby sent me some homemade granola. Talk about a win-win."

"He's a mighty fortunate man to be married to a woman like Ruby," Cameron said with a wide grin. "God sure did bless my brothers and me in that department."

"Your brother is the town doctor?" Noah asked, still trying to wrap his head around the cast of characters who lived in this town. He already knew Cameron's brother Boone was the sheriff of Love, but he hadn't known about Liam. It was evident that Liam was married to Ruby. Based on this conversation, Sophie had seen him as a patient, and there didn't appear to be anything romantic going on. Noah felt the tight sensation in his chest loosening.

"Yes," Cameron said with a nod. "One of my brothers is the town doctor. That's Liam. My other brother, Boone, is the sheriff. And Jasper, my grandfather, is the town mayor." He leaned back in his chair and smiled. "And my baby sister, Honor, runs the wildlife center."

"Quite a family," Noah said, letting out a low whistle.

Hazel returned with a steaming mug of

coffee for Sophie. "He's not even telling you about his fabulous sisters-in-law, Ruby and Gracie. And let's not forget Cam's wife, Paige. She's one in a million."

"The Prescott family is one of the founding families of Love," Sophie said in a gushing tone. "In a week or so we're going to celebrate Founder's Day in a big way. Fireworks. Festivities. Sleigh rides. It's going to be a can't-miss event. So put it on your calendar, Noah."

His calendar. Noah didn't really do social engagements. Back in Seattle he'd devoted most of his time to Catalano Security. In his off time, he met up with friends, and on the rare occasion went out on a date. But his heart really wasn't into dating, not since Kara had broken his heart and shattered his faith in women. Sometimes it felt as if he was just going through the motions.

If you don't put yourself out there, you'll never know what you're missing. His mother's voice buzzed in his ears, reminding him that there was a whole world to explore. For the past few years he had avoided putting himself out there. He didn't like to think of Kara very often, but he knew his past relationship with her served as a barrier for him getting close to another woman and trusting people in general.

At one point in time Noah had envisioned Kara as his future wife. He'd loved her, and believed she loved him in return. He had even started looking at rings in anticipation of asking her to marry him.

It had all been a lie. Kara's feelings for him had proved to be fickle. She had dumped him for a wealthy hedge fund CEO after telling Noah she wanted to be with a more ambitious and financially stable partner. Noah's aspirations of opening a security company had been dismissed by Kara, who hadn't seen it as a viable business. A rich socialite, she had been way out his league, a fact she had made very clear right before tossing him aside for another man and shattering his heart in the process.

It didn't hurt as much now to think of her, but for far too long Noah had allowed Kara's actions to dictate his life. That had to change.

As long as he was here in Love, Alaska, he was going to make the most of as many experiences as he could. And that included attending a Founder's Day celebration.

"I'll definitely put it on my calendar," he said, surprising himself by feeling a burst of enthusiasm at the idea of spending time with the citizens of this quaint hamlet.

The arrival of the first customers of the day put an end to their coffee klatch. Noah beat a path to the kitchen, where he put on his apron and began prepping his work area. Within a few minutes, his first order arrived and he set about the business of preparing breakfast for the customers.

About an hour into the morning service, Cameron popped his head into the kitchen.

"Hey, Noah. Would you mind coming out front to talk to a customer? He wants to rave about your breakfast omelet."

"Sure thing," Noah replied. "Just give me a minute."

Every now and again, Cameron asked him to come out from the kitchen so he could greet an appreciative patron or answer a question about an ingredient. He had to admit, the folks in Love were a friendly bunch who loved to compliment the cook.

The moment he entered the dining area, his gaze honed in on Sophie. Although he tried to tell himself it was only because her fiery red hair drew him in like a beacon, he knew it wasn't that simple. She was off-limits in every way conceivable, but there was something about her that tugged at him.

His stomach clenched at the sight of her standing in the middle of a group of four men, who seemed to be competing for her attention. She seemed to be enjoying it, judging by the sound of her tinkling laughter and the way she tilted her head in a playful manner.

He had no idea why, but it bugged him. Not just a little bit, either. He was fighting the urge to walk over to the table and whisk Sophie away from the salivating men. A part of his brain registered the fact that they weren't actually salivating, while another part of him felt certain they were.

And it annoyed him to no end that she seemed to be encouraging it. Perhaps this was the side of Sophie that Sussex had described. The Sophie who'd been able to ditch her fiancé without a hint of remorse. Maybe she'd been bored with her fiancé and had wanted to play the field before settling down.

Noah turned away from her and her group of admirers. He greeted the smiling customer, Eli Courtland, who regularly came to eat breakfast with his wife at the Moose Café. After accepting Eli's hearty compliments, Noah turned back toward the kitchen.

A flash of titian hair in his peripheral vision drew his attention. He couldn't help but take another look at the spectacle taking place a few feet away.

"Neanderthals," he mumbled under his breath, as he watched one man reach out and press a kiss on Sophie's hand. Noah rolled his eyes. From the looks of it, Sophie could be one of those women who enjoyed twisting men around her little finger.

For the first time in his professional life, Noah felt conflicted about passing on information to a client. Did Sussex really need to know this type of information? Noah let out a sigh. With each and every day, this assignment was getting trickier to pull off. Sophie wasn't actually doing anything noteworthy, other than living her life. But he could see that she was a much-beloved figure in this town, and clearly sought after by the men in Love. If Sussex's goal was to win Sophie back, his plan would turn to mush if she fell for someone else. Perhaps Noah's client needed this information as soon as possible. Ripping a Band-Aid off really quickly might hurt something fierce, but it was better than slowly pulling it off and prolonging the agony.

It would be a bummer if his assignment ended early, but Noah owed Sussex his truthful assessment of the situation.

Cameron sidled up to him and jerked his chin in Sophie's direction. "Now see? If you were an official participant in Operation Love, you'd be right in the thick of that." Cameron's grin threatened to overtake his entire face. "Instead of looking at things from the outside."

Noah scoffed. "Who says I want to be in the thick of a bunch of grown men competing for one woman's attention? I have zero interest in what's going on over there." He tried to make his tone nonchalant.

"Well, someone forgot to tell your face that," Cameron quipped. "You look as if you can't keep your eyes off them."

"You're imagining things," he said through gritted teeth.

"Whatever you say," Cameron replied in a singsong voice.

Noah made his way back to the kitchen without looking in Sophie's direction. As it was, he had plenty of information for his report to Sussex. Strangely, it didn't make him feel good. Instead, he noticed a gnawing sensation in his gut.

He shoved that aside, refusing to feel guilty for doing his job. Noah had a professional duty to provide his client with any and all information regarding Sophie. He wasn't in the habit of sugarcoating things.

Then why did he feel so conflicted about passing this information along to Sussex?

After reaching for his next ticket, he found himself placing the frying pan down on the stove with an extra bang. He couldn't waver about this assignment or his obligations to Sussex. To do so would indicate weakness. The past had taught him the dangers of allowing himself to veer off course. Bad things happened when you allowed any hint of emotion to creep into your investigation. Sussex was his client. His fee would rescue Noah's company from the brink of disaster. As far as Noah could tell, Sophie seemed to be content and happy with her new life in Alaska.

There was not a single thing he should feel guilty about.

All morning Sophie had been battling a wave of homesickness so strong she wasn't sure she would be able to withstand it. Right in the middle of her shift she had to suppress the urge to make a phone call to her father. She had been missing him more than usual lately, as well as the rest of her extended family. Aunt Lillian was the closest thing in this world she had to a mother figure. Other than Hazel, of course.

Ever since Sophie's beloved mother had passed away when she was a young girl, she'd missed her something fierce. Missing her father was something completely different, mainly because she knew there was something she could do to change the situation. All it would take was a single phone call. It wouldn't be a cure-all for the situation, but perhaps it would serve to bridge the gap between them. Maybe then her heart wouldn't feel as if someone had ripped out a portion of it.

What if something happened to Daddy? What if she never got to see him again? She'd heard stories about people who were estranged for years, until one of the parties passed away before fences could be mended. That would be devastating! She wasn't sure if she could live with herself if something like that happened.

Forgiveness was a healing balm. Hadn't Mama taught her that very lesson when she was a little girl? Sophie let out a sigh. She'd been working toward forgiving him, but she hadn't quite been able to move past his betrayal. It had broken her heart to realize that her father considered his only child to be expendable. Even when she'd told him about John's duplicity, he'd still urged her to go through with the wedding. All so the mighty Java Giant empire wouldn't be adversely affected. As if the shareholders even cared about her marrying her father's right-hand man, John Sussex. As if they would be tainted by the scandal of a broken engagement.

There was a part of her that worried about her father finding her and pressuring her to marry John. Even after all this time she knew her ex-fiancé hadn't given up on her or his quest to marry into the Mattson fortune. After all, he had devoted years to pursuing her and putting a ring on her finger. Being in Love had given her the strength to stand on her own two feet and to resist those type of pressures. God had been her constant companion and she'd drawn strength from Him. Running away to Alaska had given her a way out. She would always be grateful for that escape hatch.

Dear Lord, please help me find a way to bridge the gap between my father and me. I love him so very much. He hurt me badly, but I need to forgive him. I need to move past the pain and find a way to reach out to him. Because I miss him. I miss talking to him and seeing his face and hearing him call me Peaches. I've grown up here in Alaska. I'm not the same young woman I used to be. I'm wiser. Stronger. And even though I love being here in Love, I know now that I didn't need to run away to stand on my own two feet.

Sophie picked up the food sitting at the pass-through window and made her way to her customer's table. "Here you go, Zachariah," she said, setting the plate in front of him. "A turkey burger with all the trimmings and extra honey mustard. And some sweet potato fries."

Zachariah Cummings grinned at her. He

was an older, white-haired gentleman who thoroughly enjoyed his daily meals at the Moose Café. It hadn't escaped Sophie's notice that Zachariah was a lot more pleasant these days, ever since he'd been reunited with his long-lost granddaughter, Annie. Annie Murray had come to Love to run the town's public library and to find her family roots. Happily, she had found love with Declan O'Rourke.

"Thank you, sweet Sophie. I hope it tastes as good as it smells. This new cook is really something."

"Yep. He sure is," Sophie said, trying to make her voice sound neutral. The last thing she wanted was for anyone to pick up on the tiny crush she was developing for Noah. It probably was nothing more than being in the presence of a very attractive single man for long periods of time. It was the first time she'd felt this way since she'd arrived in Love.

Sophie walked over to Hazel, who was

serving her favorite customer, Jasper. Once the older woman had placed the plate in front of him, she turned around and let out a low whistle. Her eyes were as wide as saucers. Sophie frowned, then followed Hazel's gaze. It led straight to Noah, who had emerged again from the kitchen in order to talk to a customer. It made Sophie happy to see Noah interacting with the townsfolk. The residents of Love had accepted him and his cooking with open arms. She didn't want to examine her feelings too closely, or wonder why her stomach did flip-flops whenever Noah's name was mentioned.

"Noah sure is something else. He's about as easy on the eyes as a sky full of stars." Hazel jabbed her in the side. "Don't you think he's the bee's knees?"

Sophie eyed her friend warily. She knew the signals that suggested Hazel was up to something. Matchmaking flowed in her veins. She was at her happiest when the citizens of Love were paired up.

Sophie nodded. "He seems like a good guy. He's hardworking, that's for sure. And he can cook like nobody's business. Cameron made a good decision in hiring him."

"A man who cooks as if it's an art form is pure gold." Hazel sent her a glance filled with meaning. "The ladies will be lining up to meet him. You should get first dibs, since you work together. Don't even try to tell me you don't find him attractive."

Sophie's heart fluttered. "I can't think of a single woman who wouldn't," she admitted. "He's a bona fide hunk."

"Then shake a tail feather, Sophie. Invite him to a social gathering or church services," Hazel urged. "Who knows? Maybe he can be your date to my wedding."

Sophie felt her cheeks getting flushed. "I—I don't know. We work together. That could be a recipe for disaster."

Hazel waved her hand dismissively. "That doesn't amount to a hill of beans in the great scheme of things. If you don't stop putting up roadblocks, you're going to be the last single woman in town."

"Leave Sophie alone and stop carrying on about the new cook. You should be ashamed of yourself! You're old enough to be his mother." Jasper scowled up at Hazel from his table.

The woman beamed. "Yes, indeed. He's a young 'un. But there's nothing wrong with these eyes of mine. He's still an Alaskan hottie," she said in a jubilant voice. She winked at Sophie. "And a single one at that."

"If you keep carrying on like this, you might be single, too," Jasper grumbled, before digging into his omelet.

"It's too late to turn back now," Hazel said. "We've got a date with Pastor Jack in less than four weeks. I've already bought my wedding dress, so by hook or by crook, we're getting hitched."

Jasper flashed Hazel an irresistible smile. "I'm counting down the days. I can't wait to make you Mrs. Jasper Prescott."

"Oh, you say the sweetest things," Hazel said in a cooing tone. "That is, when you're not being ornery and a thorn in my side."

Sophie had to place her hand over her mouth to hide her gigantic grin. Hazel and Jasper were something else! Squabbling one minute, then making up the next. She never knew what to expect from them. She had the feeling their marital union would never be dull.

Hazel wiggled her eyebrows at Sophie. "Am I right, or am I right, Sophie? That new cook is hotter than the griddle he cooks on."

Just as Sophie thought Jasper might succumb to apoplexy, the sound of a throat being cleared drew her attention to Noah, who had made his way over without them noticing his approach. He was standing right behind Hazel, and the glint in his sky blue eyes left no doubt that he'd overheard her.

Noah's grin threatened to overtake his entire face. He locked gazes with Sophie, who couldn't have looked away if she tried.

"So what do you think, Sophie? Is Hazel right about me?" Noah asked, his eyes twinkling with mischief.

Chapter Five

Noah wanted to laugh out loud at the startled expression on Sophie's face. She resembled a deer caught in the headlights. She opened her mouth to speak, then closed it without uttering a word. She reached up and nervously smoothed back strands of her hair. She shifted from one foot to another.

"What are you doing? Fishing for a compliment, Nicholas?" Jasper barked from his seated position. He glared at Noah as if he wanted to fight him. Noah had the distinct impression Jasper didn't like him, although he wasn't quite sure why. It wasn't as if he'd done a single thing to alienate the man.

"His name is Noah," Hazel corrected.

Noah had never met anyone quite like the mayor of Love. Although everyone here in town seemed to adore the feisty gentleman, so far Noah hadn't really seen anything other than a cantankerous old man with a sharp tongue.

Hazel rolled her eyes toward the ceiling. She shook her head. "Don't mind him, Noah. He's just a tad jealous of good-looking younger men," she said in a loud whisper.

"Jealous!" Jasper sputtered. "I've never been jealous a day in my life."

"Ha! That's a laugh!" Hazel slapped her knee with her hand. "You had a conniption fit when Zachariah asked me to dance at the spring festival."

As Hazel and Jasper began to go back and forth, Noah raised his eyebrows in Sophie's direction. Did they always argue like this? he wondered. Sophie didn't seem fazed by it.

"I—I have to go check on my customer,"

she blurted, then raced toward a table by the window.

Noah had the distinct impression that his playful question had caused her to take off like a jackrabbit. He had just been teasing her. He prayed his words hadn't made her feel uncomfortable, especially since they were coworkers. As the owner of his own company, he knew that employees had to be careful not to step across any inappropriate lines.

Noah tried to stuff down the smidgen of disappointment he felt about Sophie running off. Talking to her meant discovering new things about her. And in order to keep Sussex apprised about the goings-on in Sophie's life, Noah needed to have a relationship with her.

Noah made his way back to the kitchen, chastising himself for his attempt at flirting with Sophie. Even though he knew it wasn't a wise thing to do, he hadn't been able to resist. He liked the way her creamy skin flushed and the way her lashes flickered as she tried to hide her embarrassment.

Hmm. So far, there really wasn't much he didn't like about Sophie. Except for the fact that she was the woman who'd caused his client a world of hurt and pain. Why did he always have a tendency to forget that brutal fact? It wasn't wise for him to push certain details to the side. Doing that once before had caused him to be blindsided in the worst way possible. Noah was determined not to let that happen again.

Yes, indeed. He let out a low whistle. Things were quickly becoming complicated.

This woman was dangerous to his equilibrium. Sure, she was beautiful. He'd known it before he had stepped foot in this one-of-a-kind Alaskan village. But he hadn't expected to feel such a powerful attraction to the gorgeous redhead. And her Southern accent was downright adorable. Strange how Sussex had neglected to mention her Georgia roots. He'd led Noah to believe that Sophie was a New Yorker through and through.

Nothing in his experience could ever have prepared him for her.

Noah let out a beleaguered sigh. With every smile and cutesy anecdote, she made him forget the sole reason he had ventured to Love, Alaska. She made him believe that she was an apple-pie-eating, butter-wouldn't-melt-in-her-mouth, sweet girl next door.

According to his client, that couldn't be further from the truth. Sussex had depicted her as thoughtless and cruel, self-absorbed and ditzy.

In Noah's humble opinion, Sophie didn't seem like any of those things. *But you barely know her*, he reminded himself. *First impressions aren't always correct. Sometimes you have to peel back a person's layers to really and truly see them.* Hadn't Kara shown him that in no uncertain terms?

Cameron's voice broke into his reverie. He had sneaked up on him in the kitchen when he'd been daydreaming. "Hey, Noah. I keep forgetting to tell you about our Taste of Love event. It's happening in a few days. Has anyone mentioned it to you?"

"Can't say that anyone has," Noah answered, eager to hear about it. It was a funny thing to admit, even to himself, but this town was growing on him by leaps and bounds. He was beginning to feel a part of this tight-knit community. Faces were becoming more familiar to him and people were calling out to him in the street when they crossed paths. He'd been invited to bake sales, church services, birthday celebrations and a Dr. Seuss party at the library.

"It's a town event we've been having for the last few years to help support local businesses. For instance, the bookstore might give out bookmarks and have authors do book signings, while the candy store might give out small bags of jelly beans."

"Great way to market your products," Noah said with an approving nod.

"Business has been booming here, but we still have some growing to do," Cameron said. "The event will be good for us."

"So what's on the agenda for the Moose Café?" Noah asked.

"Actually, I was hoping we could brainstorm a bit, since you're the one who's in charge of the grub. I want to do some mini coffee drinks and put Sophie in charge of that. I'll give you free rein to come up with an appetizer or two to feature at the event."

"So would Sophie and I be working together?" Noah asked. He wasn't so sure it would be a good idea to be working side by side with her. As far as he was concerned, it might be too close for comfort.

"Yes. Is there a problem with that?" Cameron asked, his brows knitting together.

As Noah struggled to honestly answer the question, a child's voice cried out, "Daddy!"

A little girl, who appeared to be around two years old, came running toward them with outstretched arms. Cameron's face lit up as he bent and lifted the little charmer into his arms. With her dark hair and chubby cheeks, she was a miniature version of Noah's boss.

"Emma!" Cameron greeted her by nuzzling her cheek with his nose. She let out a delighted cry.

"I missed you," Emma said in a soft voice. She stuck her lip out.

Cameron pressed a kiss on her cheek. "I always miss you, pumpkin."

"Emma." A beautiful blonde woman appeared in the doorway. She shook her finger at the child. "It isn't nice to run away from Mama."

Emma tugged on her father's chin. "I wanted to see Daddy."

Cameron shook his head at her. "You gotta listen to Mama. Trust me. She knows best."

The woman turned toward Noah and stuck out her hand. "Hello. I'm Paige, Cameron's wife and Emma's mother. You must be Noah. I've heard a lot about you."

"Pleased to meet you, Paige," he said, shaking her hand. He waved at Emma. "Hey there, cutie."

Emma hid her face in her father's shoulder. Noah reached out and tickled her arm. She let out a shriek of laughter, then said, "Again." Noah tickled her a few more times, much to the child's delight. Her giggles reached inside his chest and tugged at a place he hadn't even known existed.

"You're a natural with kids," Paige said, her words making Noah feel as if he was ten feet tall.

"I have a few nieces and nephews," he acknowledged. *But I'd love one of my own, truth be told.* He didn't say the words out loud. Noah simply allowed them to marinate.

After a few minutes his boss excused himself and went out into the dining area with Paige and Emma. Noah couldn't resist watching them as they settled at a table. Cameron reached out to hold his wife's hand as his daughter climbed up into his lap. The love they shared shone like a beacon.

Noah couldn't stop staring at Cameron and his amazing family. What must it be like, he wondered, to belong to someone and to bring a new life into being? For so long now it had been Noah against the world. He had deliberately set up barriers so that no woman could come close to breaking down his defenses. He'd spent so much time laying the foundation for Catalano Security that he had neglected his personal life in the process.

How many times had friends attempted to set him up on dates since Kara? More than he could count on two hands. For the most part he'd always said no. And the few times he had agreed to go, Noah had always found fault with the women. Too tall. Too short. Overly talkative. Not personable enough. So many excuses to avoid getting close to anyone.

Being back in Alaska made him yearn for things he didn't have in his life. A woman to love and be loved by. A place to call home. Comforting arms when the slings and arrows of life became too much to bear. Seattle was where he lived. It wasn't a home.

Although he'd had rumblings before about his lifestyle, these feelings had become stronger and stronger with each passing day. Being here in Love was changing him. And he couldn't help but wonder if the presence of a red-haired waitress was a big part of the transformation.

By the time Noah's shift was over, all he could think about doing was heading back to his place and taking a hot shower.

Later that evening, after he had eaten dinner and watched a little television, his cell phone rang. Noah let out a groan as he glanced at the caller ID. Sussex! He had completely forgotten he'd scheduled a phone call with him to discuss any new developments regarding his assignment.

The moment he picked up, Sussex snapped, "I was expecting your call."

"My apologies. I worked a late shift."

"Anything new to report?" The man's voice was full of tension.

Noah hesitated a moment before replying. He still wasn't sure what he intended to tell Sussex about Sophie. Although he was honor bound to report back to the man who was paying for his services, he only had to give him the facts. Nothing more.

"Catalano? Are you still there?" his client barked from the other end of the line.

"I'm still here," he said. "And I really don't have much to report. Sophie's life mainly consists of working at the Moose Café six days a week. She hasn't gone out on any dates since I've been here. Although she did express an interest in getting married and settling down. According to her, that's the reason she came to Love, Alaska."

Sussex sputtered. "Getting married? Settling down? She could have stayed right here in New York City and done those things with me!" he said in a raised voice.

Noah detected hurt in Sussex's voice, along with a dose of arrogance. "I can't say I blame you for feeling that way," he said. If Sophie had been his own fiancée this news would have been like pouring salt in an open would.

"So it's clear from what you've told me that Sophie is seeking a husband in that two-bit Alaskan town," Sussex huffed.

Noah bristled at the insult his client had hurled at the community of Love. "I wouldn't exactly call it two-bit. This town is full of great people and interesting places. Sophie seems to have found a home here, sir."

"Love, Alaska, is not her home! It's a temporary resting place. And you'd do well to remember that. Make no mistake about it! My goal is not only to get my fiancée back, it's to bring her back home to New York City. So, considering the fact that you're in my employ, that's your objective, too. Unless, of course, we're not on the same page." Sussex's tone sounded biting to Noah's ears. Clearly, the man didn't like being challenged on anything regarding this assignment. Or Sophie.

"I completely understand," Noah said through gritted teeth. "You're the boss." When had his client become so obnoxious? Most of the sympathy he'd been feeling for him went straight out the door. Maybe Sussex was simply one of those rich, entitled men who thought they could get whatever they wanted. Perhaps Sophie was just another thing he wanted to acquire.

"Catalano. The assignment has changed. You need to shift gears."

"Are my services no longer needed?" Noah asked, half hoping Sussex would pull the plug on the assignment.

"They're needed more than ever. The bottom line is that Sophie is looking for my replacement. I can't let that happen, not when

I still think there's a chance for us to get back together. I need you to make sure that doesn't go down."

A buzzing sound thundered in his ears. He had a feeling that this discussion was heading into uncomfortable territory.

Noah closed his eyes and pinched the bridge of his nose. "Sir, Sophie is an independent woman. I can't very well tell her not to date someone. We're not exactly close friends."

"No. You're right. Sophie would never listen to any man trying to rule her dating life," Sussex concurred. Noah had the feeling his client was pondering his options. Perhaps he was rethinking this desperate scheme.

Noah let out a sigh of relief. He hadn't relished the idea of interfering in Sophie's love life. The situation was becoming tenser by the moment. He felt sweat breaking out on his forehead. He couldn't remember feeling so conflicted about an assignment. A gut instinct told him he was getting in way over his head.

Sussex continued to speak. "Let's make this really simple, Catalano. If you pursue Sophie yourself, you'll keep all the other Operation Love participants at bay. I'm just asking you to keep her occupied until I can find a way to reunite with her. Take her out on the town. Bring her a bouquet of flowers. She really loves lilies. Romance her a little."

"That's not what you hired me for!" Noah said. How could his client ask him to do this if he truly loved Sophie? What kind of man thought this type of plan was acceptable?

"Let me know if you're not up to completing the assignment," Sussex said in a frosty voice. "I wired a substantial payment into your bank account this morning. For what I'm paying you, there are plenty other PIs who would gladly take this assignment."

Before Noah could reply, Sussex disconnected the call.

Noah found himself calling on God. He didn't know what to do. He was too far in to back out now. So much was riding on this paycheck. But he had no intention of dating Sophie simply to keep her away from other men in town. It would be dishonorable and shameful. What kind of man would he become if he sank to that level? And even though he was in Love under false pretenses, he still wanted to maintain his dignity. Doing as Sussex asked wouldn't allow that to happen.

He was beginning to think he'd already compromised himself by working with a man like Sussex. Could the guy really and truly love Sophie if he could ask his PI to date her? Noah felt incredibly conflicted. Things were spiraling out of control.

Dear Lord. I'm in big trouble here. I'm caught between a rock and a hard place. I need to follow through with this assignment so I can rescue my company. But I don't feel right about what I'm doing. And the deeper I find myself venturing down this path, the more conflicted I feel. Show me the way.

Chapter Six

It was a bright and frosty morning as Sophie made her way from her cabin toward Hazel's house down the lane. Hazel had invited all her bridesmaids to an early-morning breakfast in order to hash out some of the details for her upcoming nuptials.

Sophie shivered as a blast of cold air hit her in the face. Even though it wasn't far to the main house, she found herself wishing she owned a car. It was freezing outside. Although she didn't have her license, she had managed to get her permit. It was sitting right in her wallet, serving as a daily reminder to take the next steps toward obtaining her driver's license. It would be yet another move toward independence.

Sophie remembered her conversation with Noah about learning to drive. He didn't realize it, but his words had inspired her to get serious about doing so. Warmth shot through her as her thoughts veered toward the Moose Café's new hire. Little by little Sophie was seeing the real Noah hiding behind the tough veneer. He was kind. And smart. And each and every day, she was finding more things to like about him, even though he made her a little nervous. He seemed like such a simple man and a straight shooter. Noah served as a reminder that Sophie's life in Love had been built on one big fat lie.

Later on today she would be working side by side with him at the Taste of Love event. Cameron had signed her up to make coffee drinks at the function. Even though today was supposed to be a day off, Sophie couldn't say no to Cameron. He'd done so much for her since she had arrived in town, and if she ever needed anything he was right there to support her—much like the older brother she always wished for.

She breathed out a puff of air. It was so frigid outside she could see the mist in front of her face. At least her feet weren't cold. She looked down at her navy blue boots, the latest design from Hazel's footwear line, Lovely Boots. They kept her feet cozy and warm. Being friends with Hazel had plenty of perks. Being given the latest boots was at the top of the list.

By the time Sophie reached her destination, she was ready to come in from the biting cold. She let herself into Hazel's house without knocking or ringing the bell. Hazel didn't like guests to stand on ceremony. She insisted that her door was always open.

As soon as Sophie crossed the threshold, the smell of baked goods rose to her nostrils. Her stomach began to grumble at the thought of blackberry cobbler. In addition to her other skills, Hazel was a masterful baker. Once Sophie took off her coat and boots, she ventured toward the parlor, following the sound of voices.

Hazel's parlor was filled with joyful, smiling faces. Despite the early hour, the space vibrated with energy. Sophie received a hearty welcome from the other bridesmaids—Grace Prescott, Annie O'Rourke, Ruby Prescott and Paige Prescott.

No sooner had Sophie dug into a plateful of blackberry cobbler than Hazel commanded everyone's attention by a loud clearing of her throat.

"Thank you, ladies, for gathering here so bright and early on a Saturday morning," Hazel announced as she poured steaming cups of tea from her vintage floral tea set. Even the smell of scones and muffins couldn't make up for the early hour. This morning should have been Sophie's morning to sleep in. Instead, she had trudged over here in order to help plan her friend's wedding and reception.

Annie hid a yawn behind her hand. "Sure thing, Hazel. Anything for you."

Grace took a long sip of tea, then placed her cup back on the saucer. "I don't care how early it is. It's nice to get away from the house while Boone is watching Eva." She let out a little giggle. "Just the thought of him changing her diaper makes me grin."

All the ladies laughed along with her.

"Liam is fortunate. Aidan likes to sleep in now, as well," Ruby chimed in, looking at her watch. "I'm guessing those two will sleep for hours." With her mocha skin and warm brown eyes, Ruby was a stunning woman. Even better, she was down-to-earth and as sweet as pie.

"I'm happy to be sitting down for a change. I love working at the Moose, but my feet ache from standing up all day every day," Sophie said, flexing her ankles.

Hazel stood up from her seat and loudly

clapped her hands. "I was trying to wait for Honor to get here, but I can't contain myself much longer. I promised you ladies I would show you the dresses you'll be wearing at the ceremony. They finally came in from Anchorage."

"Oh, I can't wait to see them," Paige said, her expression radiating excitement. Sophie smiled over at her. Of all the ladies in the room, Paige was the only one who fit the title of fashionista.

Honor Prescott burst in the door, shaking snow off her shoulders as she took off her coat and hung it on Hazel's coatrack. "Sorry I'm late," she called out. "The roads from the wildlife center were coated with ice. I had to drive really slowly."

"Safety first. Come on in." Hazel beckoned with a wave of her hand. "Take a seat and grab some food. I'm about to unveil the bridesmaid dresses."

Honor quickly settled next to Sophie and began helping herself to breakfast. Sophie filled Honor's glass with orange juice while her friend helped herself to a muffin and hash browns.

"You arrived just in time," Hazel told Honor, then reached down into a box, pulled out a dress and held it up in front of her. It was a lavender-colored gown with feathers at the hem. Hazel's expression radiated pure joy and satisfaction. "Ta-da! What do you think, ladies? Is this elegant or what?"

Honor sputtered on her orange juice. "Oh, please, no," she said in a low voice.

"I— It sure is vibrant," Sophie said, struggling to find something positive to say.

"Isn't it, though? And who doesn't look good in purple," Hazel crowed.

"Are all the dresses just like that one?" Grace asked. The look of horror on her face didn't escape Sophie's notice.

"They are," Hazel said, looking as proud as a peacock. "So who wants to try it on?" she asked, glancing around the table.

No one spoke for a minute. Not wanting

to hurt Hazel's feelings, Sophie jumped up from her seat. "I'll try it on, Hazel. After all, lavender is one of my favorite colors."

Ruby stood up. "Me, too. If you need someone else to try it on, I'm game."

The women all nodded their heads and chimed in with their support. It warmed Sophie's insides to see the overwhelming support for Hazel. It didn't matter that the dress was hideous. Not in the grand scheme of things. Hazel was the heart and soul of Love. She was the most supportive and fiercely protective person Sophie had ever known. Although everyone called her Hazel to her face, she was often affectionately referred to as "Mama Bear" behind her back.

"You gals really are something else," Hazel said. Sophie thought she saw tears pooling in her friend's eyes. Although Hazel considered herself to be a stoic Alaskan, she was a teddy bear at her center.

"Right back atcha," Sophie said, tears welling up in her own eyes as the realization hit her that Hazel was the closest thing to family she had. Even though there was a space in her heart yearning for home, she'd found something incredible here in Love. And every single person in this room had been a part of her journey.

Hazel threw her head back and let out a cackle of laughter. For a few moments she clutched her stomach and couldn't seem to stop.

"Are you all right, Hazel?" Honor asked, her eyes wide with alarm.

Hazel swatted at her own eyes with the back of her hand. "You ladies never fail to amaze me. I wouldn't have you girls wear this monstrosity if it were the last dress on earth. I'm sorry. I know it's not April Fools' Day, but I couldn't resist pranking you." She waved the dress in front of her. "Unless, of course, you really do want to wear this lavender eyesore. It's been hanging at the back of my closet for decades."

Several sighs of relief could be heard in the room, along with shouts of laughter.

"I came to the realization that I want you ladies to wear something that you really love. So you're free to pick your own dress, as long as it's a nice shade of white."

"We can't wear the same color as the bride," Paige said, raising her hand to her neck in dismay. "That would be a huge fashion faux pas."

Hazel held her head high. "I'm not wearing white," she announced in a firm voice. "I've decided to wear a beautiful blush color. White tends to wash me out. And I'm a big fan of blush tones. Jasper loves the idea."

Sophie crossed her hands in front of her. "I think you're going to be a lovely bride, my friend." She took a few steps toward Hazel and wrapped her in a tight embrace.

"My sweet Sophie. This town sure was blessed the moment you arrived," Hazel said as she patted her back.

"Anything I've given to this town I've gotten back tenfold," Sophie said, knowing with a deep certainty the veracity of her words. Love had given her a soft place to land at a time when the bottom had fallen out of her world. She was part of this village now. And every single resident had been embedded on her heartstrings. God sure had known what He was doing when He had pointed her toward this very special place.

"Okay, this is really turning into a sob-fest," Ruby said, wiping away tears. "We're supposed to be in celebration mode."

"I know," Honor said. "Let's change the mood in here. Quick. Someone share some harmless gossip or a funny joke."

"I met the new cook at the Moose. His name is Noah," Paige said with a grin. "He's very attractive, and according to Hazel he's single."

"And ready to mingle," Hazel quipped. "Just ask Sophie. They're getting along like a house on fire."

Oohs and aahs rang out in the room. Sophie felt the heat of all their gazes.

"Come on, Sophie," Grace drawled. "Tell us all about the new cook at the Moose. And don't you dare leave out a single detail."

"Yes, please do," Ruby pleaded.

Hazel sent Sophie a knowing glance. "If I had my druthers, Sophie and Noah would be the next match in Operation Love."

Sophie swung her gaze in her direction. "Really, Hazel? We're just friends. I barely know the guy."

Hazel winked at her. "Ha! That's exactly how Jasper and I started out." She held up her fingers and made air quotes. "'Just friends.' And look at us now. We're a perfect match."

Sophie shook her head. Hazel wasn't letting this Noah thing go! And the way the other ladies were looking at her made her feel like a specimen under a microscope. They were practically salivating for any details about Noah.

She looked around the table. "Seriously. There's nothing going on between me and Noah. I mean, he's gorgeous and he can cook like nobody's business. But he's not looking to be matched up with anyone, so there's no point in even going down that road."

Sophie knew she needed to minimize any feeling she was harboring toward Noah. If these ladies sensed anything, it would be a feeding frenzy.

"So if he was interested would you give it a whirl?" Hazel asked.

Leave it to her to pose such a blunt question. Suddenly, all eyes were focused on Sophie again.

She fidgeted in her seat. "Maybe," she blurted out, surprising herself in the process. For far too long now she'd played it safe, never really putting herself or her feelings on the line. It was time to stop making excuses. Being hurt in the past didn't justify closing her heart off to romance. And if a man truly loved her, she'd like to think he would understand about her being the Java Giant heiress. Deep down, she thought it might take a special kind of man to get past her father's fortune and the fact that she was the sole heir set to inherit Roger Mattson's vast empire. Her biggest fear was that no man would ever be able to see past her father's bank balance.

"What's that saying? Love finds you when you're not really looking for it," Ruby said. "You never know what can happen."

The thought of being matched up with Noah made butterflies soar in Sophie's tummy. Was it possible that they could turn a fledgling friendship into something more romantic? The very thought made her pulse skitter with excitement. All this time she'd been dancing around becoming involved with someone here in town. She'd allowed her fears to get in the way. Sophie had put up roadblocks to her happily-ever-after.

If she was being honest with herself, she'd consider that Noah Callahan might just be her match. No other man in Love had ever given her goose bumps. And lately, when she closed her eyes at night and drifted off to sleep, Noah's face flashed in her vision.

She sucked in a deep, fortifying breath. Sophie had to be strong. Giving in to a feeling was silly. Being drawn to Noah was unfortunate because there really wasn't any way for the two of them to be together. After all, she wasn't exactly being honest about who she was and why she had chosen to hide out in Love, Alaska. And she wasn't at a place emotionally where she could trust a man.

It was such a shame. After all, God's commandment was to love one another. She was sick of living in the past, but the truth was that she wasn't over it, not by a long shot. And until those wounds healed, she would just have to stay out of the dating pond.

Noah stood in the tent on the town green looking around at the bustling crowd. He couldn't believe the number of people who had turned out for the Taste of Love event. So much for Love being a small hamlet. The event was bursting at the seams.

He had arrived early to help Cameron set up the table and hang up a sign advertising the Moose Café.

Noah had decided to prepare mini pizzas, spinach quiches and Alaskan crab cakes. He knew for a fact that Sophie was a big fan of the crab cakes. It felt a little strange knowing he was making decisions based on her likes and dislikes. And it wasn't a bad strange, either.

According to Cameron, Sophie would be making blended coffee drinks for the crowd. They would be working side by side at today's event. Noah blew out a breath of air. Perhaps too close for comfort. In the back of his mind he couldn't help but think about Sussex's demand that he court Sophie. He could practically feel his blood pressure rising just pondering it. It didn't give him a very good impression of his client.

"I'm going to head out, Noah," Cameron said. "I'd stick around and help, but I promised to take Emma to a birthday party today." He looked around the area. "Sophie should be here any minute."

"Enjoy yourself with that little sweetheart of yours. We'll be fine," Noah said. It made him happy to think of Cameron spending time with his precious daughter. In a million years Noah had never imagined he would be envious of Cameron's domestic life.

Noah wasn't alone for long. Residents began streaming into the tent and lining up for a sampling of his appetizers. Noah couldn't believe how many townsfolk greeted him by name. It felt as if he was being woven into the fabric of this quaint town, stitch by stitch. And it felt good. He never would have expected to feel so at home here.

Sophie showed up a few minutes after he began serving the crowd.

"I'm so sorry to be late, Noah," she said, looking a bit flustered as she joined him at the table. She immediately began setting up the cups, ingredients and blender. Watching her in action was akin to seeing a whirlwind.

Of course, she looked adorable, right down to her boots and the hot-pink down jacket she was wearing. She had on a pair of earmuffs and leg warmers pulled up past her boots.

"No problem. Take your time. This isn't a pressure cooker. It's a very relaxed event." He inhaled deeply, then exhaled. "Just breathe."

Sophie followed his instructions. She inhaled, exhaled, then told him, "I was at Hazel's house. She was having a gathering about her wedding." Sophie beamed. "I'm a bridesmaid."

Noah had observed the close relationship between the two women. He had to admit it was heartwarming. Surely Sophie couldn't be this terrible person if Hazel and all the residents of Love adored her. Or could she? So far Noah had seen up close and personal the way Sophie could charm birds from the trees. He needed to put up his armor today. Sophie had the ability to wear down his defenses. Every time he was in her presence, he found himself liking her more and more. And every time he spoke to Sussex, he began to lose more and more respect for him. Everything was turned upside down. More than anything else, Noah liked order. He liked for things to make sense, and with each day that passed he found himself more conflicted.

Every time he thought about Sussex asking him to date Sophie to keep her away from other men in town, he wanted to clench his fists in anger. His client radiated entitlement, which rubbed Noah the wrong way. He had tossed and turned in bed last night, disturbed by the turn the assignment had taken.

At the moment he needed to keep his

thoughts focused on Sophie and today's event. There would be plenty of time later to try to figure things out.

He grinned at her, getting a kick out of how excited she was about the upcoming nuptials. "That's pretty special, to be in the wedding. She told me to look for an invitation in the mail," Noah said, surprised that he was on the invitation list.

Given the unpredictable nature of this assignment, Noah had no idea whether he'd still be in Love to attend the wedding. The very thought of going back to Seattle didn't have as much appeal as he'd imagined it would. After all, he'd taken on Sussex's assignment in order to help his struggling company. Catalano Security still represented his hopes and dreams, as well as the livelihoods of all his employees.

And could he really sit in God's house and watch a loving couple get married, all the while knowing he was in town under false pretenses? His gut twisted with the implications of the lie he was living. Nothing he'd established here in Love was real. It had all been built on falsehoods. There was no way of getting around it.

Sophie chattered on in a chirpy voice. "It's really going to be a wonderful day, full of romance and celebration. Jasper and Hazel are this town's version of Romeo and Juliet." She had a dreamy expression on her face as she spoke about the older couple.

"I hope not," Noah teased. "Look at how they ended up."

Sophie swatted at him in a playful manner and giggled. "You know what I mean. They might fight and fuss, but they're the real deal."

As more customers streamed in, Noah and Sophie could no longer talk one on one, but they interacted with the residents as a duo. Noah would serve up an appetizer while Sophie handed each person a blended coffee beverage. Everything was running as smoothly as possible, without a single hitch. The food and drinks were a big hit.

"Hey, Dwight. How are you? Thanks for stopping by," Sophie greeted the brown-haired, bespectacled man with enthusiasm and warmth, neither of which was returned. Noah thought the new arrival looked as sour as a lemon drop candy. His eyes radiated unhappiness and a hint of despair. Noah felt a smidgen of sympathy for the nerdy resident, who was obviously not a happy camper.

Noah knew Dwight in passing, as the town treasurer with the no-nonsense attitude, and the annoying habit of leaving customer comments on his receipt at the Moose Café. Suffice it to say, they were rarely compliments. Cameron dismissed Dwight's feedback. He'd explained to Noah that the guy was a "miserable bachelor" who seemed determined to be unhappy.

"Have you heard anything from Marta?" Dwight asked Sophie. Noah couldn't help but overhear the question since he was standing mere inches away. It was obvious he had it bad for this Marta woman. There was a desperate quality to his voice and he had a hangdog expression etched on his face. Noah instantly recognized the name Marta. She had been his predecessor at the Moose Café.

Sophie shook her head. "No, we haven't heard a word. I'm sorry. I wish I could tell you differently."

Dwight hung his head. "I should have known better than to put all my hopes and dreams in a woman I didn't know very well. I'm some kind of fool."

"No, you're not, Dwight. There's nothing wrong with holding on to hope," Sophie said.

He let out a sigh. "It's hard to keep hope alive when I'm still as single as a dollar bill."

"Don't worry, Dwight. She's out there. I just know it." Sophie's voice was filled with sincerity and encouragement. She was buoying him up when he appeared to be at his lowest. Noah had compassion for the man, who likely only wanted love and devotion. No doubt the cranky attitude was a facade he wore to prevent people from feeling sorry for him.

"From your lips to God's ears," Dwight said in a low voice.

Noah handed a plate of appetizers to a scrawny teenager, then turned to Dwight. He couldn't help but add his two cents' worth. "You're no different than most of us. At the end of the day, we all want to be happy, preferably with a partner by our side."

Dwight blinked at him with surprise. There was a world of pain resting in his eyes. "Yes. That's very true. We weren't meant to walk through this world alone."

"We most definitely were not," Noah concurred, thinking about his parents and their forty years of marital bliss.

Dwight seemed like a good egg, he realized. Sometimes appearances were deceiving.

"And I know you're lonely, but you're not always going to feel this way. It's just a passing thing," Sophie added. "I get lonely sometimes when I think about being so far away from home, but then I focus on how the townsfolk in Love always treat me like I was born and bred here. That's an awesome cure for loneliness. Surround yourself with people who care about you."

Dwight nodded. "Thanks. I'm going to listen to your advice. This town does have a lot to offer. I take that for granted sometimes." After quickly downing a coffee drink, he headed away toward another booth.

Sophie's gaze trailed after him. She resembled a mama bird watching her baby leave the nest. "Dwight won't truly be happy until he finds his match," she said in a low voice. "He needs someone to give him some pointers in the romance department."

"Like a tutor?" Noah asked with a chuckle.

Sophie's face lit up. Her green eyes flashed.

"Yes!" she cried out. "Exactly. What a great idea, Noah."

Noah couldn't take his eyes off Sophie. Everything about her was animated. He could almost see the wheels turning in her head regarding Dwight's situation. Something told him she wouldn't rest until her friend had his happily-ever-after. She cared about people—truly and deeply. It radiated from within her.

He felt his stomach doing somersaults. What was it about Sophie that made him feel like a teenager with his first crush? The town of Love was filled with attractive women, most of whom had come to town due to the Operation Love campaign. They were all looking for love and companionship. Some of them had even come into the Moose Café to flirt with him. Yet all he could see was Sophie. It was more than her good looks. He supposed it boiled down to simple chemistry. The laws of attraction. Something you couldn't really put your finger on.

He felt a slight pang in the region of his heart. If he was smart, he would pack his bags and head home on the next thing smoking. But he knew it would only complicate his life back in Seattle if he bailed on the assignment and lost much-needed salary. Noah was in the middle of a tug-of-war—his budding feelings for Sophie versus his obligation to save his company and his employees from financial ruin.

Noah had known before he ever stepped foot in Love that Sophie was capable of twisting men around her finger. Perhaps he was just another man who'd fallen for her charms. The past had him in its grip, reminding him of the way he'd been taken in by a woman once before. Kara had shown him in no uncertain terms that he wasn't always the best judge of a woman's character.

He needed to stay focused on the reason he had traveled to this small fishing village in Alaska in the first place. Getting caught up in Sophie's web could prove to be disastrous, not only for the future of Catalano Security, but for his heart.

Chapter Seven

Sophie felt a surge of triumph flow through her veins at the sight of Noah helping himself to another one of her coffee drinks. She felt a huge grin tugging at her lips. She vividly remembered him telling her how he didn't drink coffee. Score! Sophie had the feeling her mochaccino had made a believer out of him. It was the yummiest drink she created at the Moose Café. Customers ordered it in droves.

Her father would get a big kick out of this story, Sophie realized with a sinking feeling. He loved hearing tales of people who had been converted to drinking coffee. It was moments such as this one when she missed him like nobody's business. Roger Mattson was far from perfect. He tended to focus too much on Java Giant and business meetings and his vast empire. But he always said he loved her more than anything else in his world, including his corporation. Sophie wished she could believe it. Maybe then it would be easier to forgive him and bridge the gap between them.

She wrapped her arms across her chest. "I'm f-freezing," she said. Cameron had placed little heaters inside the tent so they wouldn't turn into Popsicles, but it was still bone-chillingly cold.

"Just keep moving around," Noah advised her. "Then you won't feel it as much. The crowd is starting to thin out. Only a half hour more to go."

Sophie began walking back and forth in front of their stand. Then she began doing jumping jacks. She felt the intensity of

Noah's gaze. Truthfully, she wasn't sure if he was checking her out or marveling at her silliness.

As the clock ticked down, they serviced the last of the crowd, then began packing up the leftover items. Despite the frigid temperature, the time had flown by.

"By the way, Sophie, I hope that I didn't make you uncomfortable the other day at work," Noah said, his voice full of apology. "I only meant to tease you about Hazel's comment. Sorry if my sense of humor made you cringe."

"No. Not at all," she said, right before correcting herself. "Well, actually, maybe just a little, but I'm a bit on the shy side, so it doesn't take much to make me blush."

Noah began to chuckle, creating little creases at the sides of his mouth. His blue eyes twinkled.

"What's so funny?" Sophie asked.

"You don't really seem all that shy. I mean, sometimes you do, but for the most part you're bubbly and personable. There doesn't seem to be a single customer you don't chat with as if they're your best friend. Honestly, you seem like a classic extrovert."

Sophie felt flattered that he had noticed all these things about her. It made her feel ten feet tall. "I think that's the Southern gal in me, if I'm being honest. Back in Saskell, I used to be a quiet little mouse until my mama taught me a big lesson. She told me that I was her ray of sunshine and it would make her the happiest mama in the world if I could spread that sunshine wherever I went. It was her way of helping me come out my shell, but she made me believe I was doing something for her. And I would have done anything to make Mama smile."

"You must miss her a lot."

Emotion clogged Sophie's throat. It was never easy to let people know her mother was no longer with her. "More than you know, Noah. She passed away when I was small. She was everything a girl could ever want or need in a mom. I think a mother is really the heart of the home. And when she died nothing was ever quite the same. The sparkle was gone. I think a lot of the miscommunication between my father and me stems from that loss…that void. We never managed to fill it up. My parents were divorced, but they never stopped loving each other. My daddy and I both grieved her loss, but as time went by, we did it independent of each other. We didn't lean on one another." Sophie's eyes pooled with tears. "But I do believe that I carry her around with me every single day. We don't ever lose the person's essence. It's ingrained in us."

"I agree with you. My gram passed away two years ago. I think about her all the time. She taught me how to make my famous meatballs and gravy."

"Well, she did a great job. It's already spread all over town that your meatballs are scrumptious." Sophie rubbed her hand across her stomach. "One of these days I'm going to sit down at a table at the Moose and order a huge serving of them. No pasta. No bread. Just meatballs."

"I'd love to see that." Noah threw his head back and laughed. "This town is something else. Word of mouth sure travels fast here."

"Like the speed of sound," Sophie said in a playful tone. "That has its drawbacks, of course, when the news isn't so favorable. Or when it's of a gossipy nature."

Noah scrunched up his nose as if he smelled something bad. "I imagine so. There are gossips in every town. Sadly, bad news tends to travel faster than good news."

"Is Love different from where you grew up in Alaska?" Sophie couldn't contain her curiosity about Noah's origins. There was a little hint of mystery that surrounded him.

"Very different," he said with a nod. "I grew up in Homer. The population is much larger, and it has a different vibe. This town has an old-fashioned charm. I almost feel like I've stepped back in time here in Love.

What they share is a great sense of community. Back home people chip in and help each other when we need it the most."

"It must have been amazing to grow up in Alaska," Sophie said, as images of a pint-size Noah flashed before her eyes.

Noah grinned, showcasing his dimples. "It was pretty close to perfection," he admitted. "It's what I'd like to give my kids one day. The great outdoors as a playground. Strong family values. Siblings to make things interesting. An appreciation of the simple treasures in life."

Sophie smiled as images of dark-haired little children came to her. She didn't say it out loud, but she would have loved a sibling or two. It would have been nice to walk through childhood with a brother or sister.

"Are you hungry?" Noah asked. "Taste of Love has been pretty amazing, but I'm starving."

"Truthfully, I'm famished," Sophie admitted. "I was so busy servicing the crowd, I forgot to eat anything."

"Well, we can't have that, can we? I don't think Cameron would mind if I whipped something up for us over at the Moose." Noah gestured toward the packaged-up supplies. "We have to take these boxes back there, anyway. He gave me the keys to lock up the place."

"Cameron wouldn't mind one bit if we ate a little something. He's one of the most generous men on the planet."

"He's a good guy. So far he's shown me nothing but kindness," Noah said.

Sophie nodded enthusiastically. "There's an abundance of that in this town, isn't there?"

"Yep. There sure is," Noah agreed. "It astounds me every time I hear someone calling to me from across the street, or asking me over to dinner because they think I might be lonely. I've never known a place quite like this before. It's almost as if there are no strangers here."

Sophie beamed with pride. Yes, indeed. This town was one-of-a-kind. She was now officially a resident of Love, Alaska, since she'd lived here for over a year. It made her happy to know Noah was getting acclimated to the community she loved so much. This town was good for him. He was opening up more and more every day. Noah was allowing light to shine on him rather than hiding himself away behind a somber disposition.

Sophie wanted him to stay here in Love and continue to work at the Moose Café alongside her, Hazel and Cameron. More than anything, she wanted to continue to get to know Noah better. It wasn't simply because he was a nice person, either. Sophie was beginning to suspect that Noah Callahan might be one of the most wonderful newcomers that Love, Alaska, had ever welcomed to town.

* * *

Noah and Sophie loaded up his car with the leftover items. Despite her small frame, she held her own with carrying the boxes. He drove over to the Moose Café and parked in back by the kitchen door, making it easier to transfer the boxes inside.

As he unlocked the door, Noah couldn't help but think of Cameron and the way he'd simply handed over the key to him. The man trusted him, Noah realized. He didn't want to think about it for too long, or guilt would nag at him. In a few weeks he would be tendering his resignation and leaving Cameron high and dry, without a cook for his establishment. The very thought caused a tightening sensation in his belly.

For the most part, Noah conducted straightforward investigations and serviced the needs of his clients in an uncomplicated fashion. He wasn't in the business of hurting people. This time around the fallout would leave ripples all over town. That knowledge burned his insides.

He had tossed and turned last night, going over the details of his current situation with as much finesse as he could. He'd even devised an exit strategy so he could get out of town if he needed to. But he didn't think he could ditch and run. If nothing else, he liked to think that he wasn't a coward. And he couldn't imagine leaving this town without saying goodbye to everyone who'd shown him kindness.

For the moment he was going to focus on fixing dinner for himself and Sophie. He was going to live in the here and now. Later on, he would figure out how to wrap up this investigation, get paid and head back to Seattle. In the meantime, there was no harm in cooking a meal for Sophie.

"What's your favorite food?" he asked her. They were standing in the kitchen, having unloaded all the boxes and stashed the contents in the supply room.

"Grilled cheese. And french fries." Sophie clapped her hands together. He chuckled at the sight of her. At the moment she resembled a small child. "Oh, and I like pickles on the grilled cheese."

Noah wrinkled his nose. "Pickles? On a grilled cheese sandwich?"

"Hey! Don't knock it until you've tried it. It might just be your next favorite thing."

Noah found himself laughing out loud. Grilled cheese and pickles! As if he could ever enjoy that wacky combination.

He began scrubbing a bunch of potatoes, then took out a cutting board and chopped them up. When he'd placed them in a bowl, he drizzled olive oil over the lot, adding rosemary, Parmesan cheese, oregano, salt and pepper. He then placed them on a baking sheet and slid them into the oven.

"Hey! Can I do something to help?" Sophie asked eagerly.

"Sure thing." He nodded toward the fridge. "You can cut up some cheddar cheese for the sandwiches. And grab the jar of pickles while you're in there. Unless, of course, you've changed your mind about them." He made a face. "I won't hold it against you if you've decided to skip the pickles."

Sophie poked her head out from behind the fridge door, triumphantly holding up a jar. "Are you kidding me? These pickles are going to make this the best grilled cheese sandwich in the history of sandwiches."

Noah nodded approvingly. "I like your moxie. If you're going out on a limb, do it with conviction."

As Sophie began working with the block of cheese, conversation flowed easily between them. With every passing moment, Noah felt as if he was really getting to know her. And with every second that ticked by, he found himself trying to reconcile his client's portrayal of her with the charming barista in his presence. Sophie didn't seem cold or calculating. As far as he could tell she seemed genuine and sweet.

"You're obviously a natural in the kitchen. Did you always want to become a cook?" Sophie asked, a curious expression on her face.

Everything Noah had learned about cooking had come from his parents. Dee Dee and Randy Catalano had owned a diner in Homer since Noah was a kid. The Highline Diner had been his stomping grounds, the place where he'd learned to make everything from eggs Benedict to Belgian waffles to Philly cheesesteak sandwiches.

"My family owns a restaurant here in Alaska. I grew up in that environment and learned to cook at an early age." He let out a chuckle. "One of my earliest memories is learning how to make lasagna from my grandfather. He grew up in Sicily and came over to Alaska after he married my grandma. He taught me something I'll never forget. When you cook for someone, always add a special ingredient. Cook it with love."

Sophie let out a gasp. Noah watched a

myriad of expressions cross her face. Tears pooled in her eyes.

He wiped his hands on his apron and quickly made his way to her side, placing a gentle hand on her shoulder. "Hey! Are you okay? Did I say something to upset you?"

Sophie shook her head. "No. You just made me homesick for a second. My family has a similar expression." She heaved a tremendous sigh. "Being here in Love is wonderful. I feel like I've found my footing after falling on my face a few times. But not being able to see the people I love has been difficult." She pressed her hand against her chest. "My heart aches a little from missing them."

"Sounds like a perfect time to give 'em a call. The fries won't be ready for a bit, so why don't you make a phone call home? I'm sure they'd love to hear from you."

Sophie ducked her head. "I can't," she said in a soft voice. "We're not exactly on speaking terms at the moment."

He had to mask his reaction so Sophie wouldn't see his complete and utter surprise at her statement. Noah hadn't seen this curveball coming. It was incredibly difficult to imagine her estranged from anyone. She didn't seem capable of remaining at arm's length with her loved ones, even though it fit in perfectly with his client's portrayal of Sophie as cold and unfeeling. And it certainly hadn't been included in the information Sussex had provided him. Why hadn't he been told by his client that Sophie and her family were at odds?

"I don't want to pry, but is it something that can be mended?" He blurted the question, not knowing whether he was asking for himself or for his investigation.

Sophie shook her head. "Not at the moment. Hopefully someday." She began to fiddle with her fingers. "I was being pushed in a lot of different directions that weren't good for me. Strings were being pulled behind my back. When I needed my family to support me unconditionally, they didn't. And it hurt me very badly."

He took a moment to let her words sink in. Sophie's pain was palpable.

"Family dynamics are difficult sometimes. Take it from me. I have four brothers at home. Growing up, we fought and scrapped and argued. And we still do from time to time," Noah admitted. "But there's nothing we wouldn't do for each other. And I'm guessing that your family feels the exact same way about you."

Sophie bit her lip. "I used to think so, but they wanted me to marry someone who didn't want to marry me for the right reasons. When I exposed him, my father didn't believe me. He was on my ex-fiancé's side. It's kind of hard to get past something like that. It crushed me."

Everything grew hushed in the kitchen. Noah felt his entire body freeze up. Was she talking about Sussex? If so, none of it meshed with the background story Noah had been given by his client. Hadn't he said their relationship had been idyllic until Sophie had dumped him and left for Alaska? Hadn't he implied another man was involved?

"You were engaged?" Noah asked, trying to keep his voice sounding normal. He needed to figure out what was going on. Was Sophie playing him for sympathy? That didn't really make sense to him, since there was no reason for her to make up this elaborate story. After all, she had no idea he was actually a private investigator hired to keep tabs on her.

Sophie nodded. The pain etched on her face made his stomach ache. In that moment he wanted to hunt down the people who had hurt her and give them a piece of his mind. John Sussex? Her family? What had they done to this woman?

"Yes, I was supposed to get married. But I decided not to go through with the wedding once I realized he was only using me. I overheard a rather incriminating conversation between him and a lady friend of his. To tell you the truth, it was rather heartbreaking. I heard him say he didn't love me and he never had." Sophie sighed. "It's a terrible feeling to know you're a pawn in someone else's game, but it made me realize that I didn't want to be used or manipulated on such a grand scale. Not for anything in this world." She shrugged. "He'd been a close family friend for years, though, so it was a double betrayal."

Noah frowned. According to Sophie, her ex-fiancé hadn't loved her. And there had been another woman involved. She had mentioned being used. The agony on her face when she had spoken about being betrayed resonated with him. He'd walked down that twisted, winding road himself. Kara's deception still affected him to this day.

But his head felt muddled. What he'd just heard didn't mesh with his client's story that Sophie had been a disloyal fiancée who'd broken his heart and run off to Alaska. Sophie had mentioned being used as a pawn, which piqued Noah's curiosity. Why hadn't Sussex given him more background information? He needed to get to the bottom of all the inconsistencies. Quickly.

He didn't really trust himself to speak at the moment. For just a little bit, he wanted to let the information settle inside him. It was hard to accept that his professional instincts might have been way off course. It was a matter of pride with him to get facts right. In his line of work too many things could go awry if he didn't. Had financial desperation made him sloppy? Had he missed red flags with Sussex? Or was Sophie laying it on thick to win his sympathy?

"That's why I appreciate this town so much," she continued. "I came here to get away from all of the turmoil and to make a fresh start. And even though it was hard, I managed to do it."

"It sounds like you wanted to get away from all the drama," Noah said. If she was telling the truth, it was a game changer. She wasn't the femme fatale. She could possibly be the victim.

Noah turned away from the stove and looked at Sophie. In this moment he wanted to give her some advice, and it had nothing to do with his assignment or his growing attraction to her. It was just plain talk from a friend. "I do believe that there's nothing on this earth like family. I understand why you were devastated, and I'm sure there's a lot you're not saying, but maybe you should consider reaching out to your family. Give them an opportunity to make things right."

Sophie regarded him with eyes as big as an owl's. She didn't respond, but merely gave a slight nod of her head.

The ding of the buzzer alerted Noah that the french fries were ready. He grabbed a mitt and took them out of the oven, then placed the pan on the stove. With his back to Sophie, he turned on the griddle and began making the grilled cheese sandwiches, making sure to add pickles to hers. Noah felt a little smile twitching the corners of his lips as he did so. This was a first for him.

Noah was glad she couldn't see his face at the moment. He knew it must be twisted with confusion. He had no idea what to make of anything other than the fact that he was enjoying this time with Sophie. Everything flowed so nicely between them. It was comfortable and natural. He felt as if he'd known her for years.

Unfortunately, the information she'd just revealed had brought him back to the stark reality of his situation. His assignment compromised everything between the two of them. Or anything there might be. She thought he was someone she could trust. Noah felt unworthy of the information she'd just shared with him.

Had Sussex been able to pull the wool over his eyes? Had Noah's financial situation caused him to miss warning signs about his client? Had the instability of Catalano

Security caused him to lower his professional standards?

So much for his PI skills! He prided himself on being able to detect a lie. His instincts were usually on point.

Or was he simply blinded by Sophie's beauty and vast charms?

It wouldn't be the first time, he reminded himself. Kara had fooled him right up until the very end. He needed to tread carefully. So much hinged on this assignment.

After grabbing some plates and napkins, Sophie set the table. Her mouth watered at the delectable smells emanating from the kitchen. She didn't think a grilled cheese sandwich and fries had ever smelled so tantalizing.

By the time they sat down to eat, her stomach was making growling noises. Just as it appeared Noah was reaching for his sandwich, Sophie said, "Let's say grace." She watched as he bowed his head and closed his eyes, then quickly followed suit.

"Lord, thank You for this food we are about to receive from Thy bounty. Amen," Sophie said with conviction.

When she opened her eyes, Noah was looking at her with a curious expression. It seemed as if he wanted to say something. So far, Sophie had been able to deduce that he was a very introspective person. A thinker. Maybe even a little bit of an introvert. It was exciting to see him come out of his shell, bit by bit.

"Thanks for blessing the food," he said after a few beats. "I have to admit something to you. I haven't prayed over my food for quite some time." He shook his head, looking regretful. "Hearing you pray over the food reminds me of sitting down for meals with my family. I used to bless the food all the time at the dinner table. My mother made my brothers and me take turns."

"I think it's only right to thank God for

nourishment, especially when I love to eat." Sophie let out a giggle, then spread her arms wide. "It would be a shame not to thank God for all of this great food."

"Let's dig in then," Noah said, reaching for his sandwich and taking a huge bite.

The moment Sophie bit into her grilled cheese she let out a groan of appreciation. "Mmm. This is delicious. And the fries are great, too. I can't believe you baked them." Sophie dipped one into the small bowl of ketchup.

"I can't take the credit. It's Mom's recipe, right down to the secret ingredient."

"Secret ingredient, huh? Care to share?" Sophie teased. She put her finger to her lips. "I won't tell."

Noah took another big bite of his grilled cheese, chewed, then swallowed. "No can do. My mother is very serious about her cooking. I'm not going to risk the wrath of Dee Dee by spilling the beans. She's a sweetheart, unless you mess with her recipes."

"She sounds like an incredible woman," Sophie said in a gushing tone. "One of my favorite memories of my mama was making peach jam and packaging it in little glass jars. Each jar had a pretty top and they each came with a label that said Made with Love by Sophie and Mom."

"The good thing about making memories is that we never lose them. Not really. We can cherish them for the rest of our lives." Noah looked thoughtful. "I'm the only son who left Homer. My brothers are still there—two have families and help run the diner. The other two work in the area. You have no idea how many times a day I reflect upon our childhood." He pressed his palm against his chest. "All of those moments are right here. I carry them around with me wherever I go. And I can pull them out whenever I feel the need."

Sophie suddenly felt a lump in her throat. Noah had hit the nail right on the head. Memories were forever. And despite everything her father had done to hurt her, he was still the same man who had raised her. Loved her. Sheltered her in his arms when her mother died unexpectedly of pneumonia. People weren't perfect, were they? It hurt terribly to feel betrayed, but it didn't erase the love.

"Thank you," Sophie said, in a voice barely above a whisper.

Noah swung his gaze up from his plate. "For what?" he asked, confusion evident in his tone.

Sophie put her sandwich down. "For reminding me of the good times. When something bad happens we tend to focus on that particular event." Her shoulders sagged. "You're right about memories. They're snapshots of the past. Reminders of events we may have taken for granted. Christmases. Parties. Our sixteenth birthday. It wasn't all bad."

"My mother used to always say we've got

to take the bitter with the sweet." Noah put the last of his french fries in his mouth.

The bitter with the sweet. Could it really be that simple?

A year had passed and now Sophie had a little distance from the turmoil that had led her to flee New York City. John and her father were not interchangeable. John's actions had been reprehensible. Amoral. Her father had been blind to John's sins against her. He had sided with her ex-fiancé when she'd needed him to be firmly, devotedly by her side. He had chosen to believe John. It had felt like a knife in the back. It had seemed as if he'd picked business over his only child.

It still hurt terribly, but in this moment all Sophie wanted to do was forgive, the same way she would want to be forgiven. Listening to Noah made it all seem so simple. But she knew it wasn't. Sophie didn't feel like the Java Giant heiress anymore. The truth was hard to ignore. She'd never quite fit into those shoes. It had always been as if her life as Sophie Mattson was someone else's she'd been observing through a filmy window. She much preferred life as Sophie Miller—barista, waitress, transplant to Alaska.

Roger Mattson wasn't a man who would take lightly to the heir to his empire renouncing it all for a simple life in the wilds up North. Sophie bit her lip. At the moment she had both feet planted in Love, while a huge chunk of her heart remained in New York City.

Once Noah dropped Sophie back at the Black Bear Cabins she immediately changed into her pajamas and sat down with a hot cup of tea. There had been a little moment in the car where she'd thought Noah might lean over and kiss her. Just the thought of it made her toes tingle. She was probably being fanciful. Noah was the type of guy who could get any girl he wanted simply by crooking his finger.

She let out a sigh of contentment. Tonight had been very enjoyable. Today, too. Sophie loved town events and this one had been no different. Sharing it with Noah had made it extra fun and whimsical. Everything about Love was so new to him. Seeing it through his eyes reminded Sophie of her first few days as a newcomer to this quaint town. Everything had been shiny and new and straight out of a travel brochure.

Sophie had shocked herself by revealing intimate details of her past to Noah. These feelings had been bubbling up for so long and she'd managed to keep such a tight rein on them. Tonight they had just risen to the surface. Noah had been in the right place at the right time.

She had never imagined it would be so difficult to hide so many things about herself. Even though she had embraced a new life in Love, her past had shaped her. In the last year she had tripped up a time or two, but other than Grace, no one knew she was really Sophie Mattson. Not even Noah. That knowledge weighed heavily on her heart. How could she ever find love while holding so tightly to this secret? And if she did find a special someone in the future, how would she ever know if he truly loved her for herself and not the Java Giant fortune?

It had felt good to tell Noah her truths about John and her family. Sometimes it was easier to talk to someone you didn't know very well. Somehow the pressure had felt less intense. To Noah she was a blank slate. Telling him about her relationship with John felt freeing. With Noah, Sophie didn't have to worry about revealing things about her past that might disappoint or shock him. He hadn't seemed judgmental at all, or critical of her estrangement from her loved ones. He had really listened to her and then given her food for thought.

Was it really possible to just reach out and connect with her father? Or would the weight of the past come crashing down around them? Sophie suspected their estrangement was tied up in the loss of her mother, a terrible blow neither of them had ever fully recovered from. Ever since then they had been tiptoeing around each other.

There's love in the bottom of every cup. She couldn't stop thinking of the slogan she knew so well. Those words were stuck in her head, reminding her of everything she'd left behind.

A person could convince themself that they'd done the right thing, especially after a betrayal, Sophie realized. Talking to Noah about his large, bustling family had broken something loose inside her. She wasn't sure she cared about being right any longer. Missing her father was like missing a limb. She wasn't a hard-hearted person. It had taken every ounce of strength she had to keep up this huge divide between herself and the people she loved more than anything in the world.

Chapter Eight

Noah looked out the huge bay window of Cameron's house. It had snowed last night, dumping at least five inches of powder on the ground. Gazing at the wintry landscape made him smile. He felt at home here in Alaska in a way he had never experienced in Seattle. Although it was a big and beautiful city, it had never quite tugged at his heartstrings. And even though he didn't relish shoveling the driveway, it was a small price to pay for a little slice of paradise.

This morning was going to be a relaxing one for Noah. The Moose Café wasn't scheduled to open until noon due to some maintenance issues, which gave him some free time to explore the town. He let out a groan as he remembered the favor Sophie had finagled from him yesterday. A full twenty-four hours later and Noah still wasn't quite certain how he'd managed to get roped in to serving as Dwight's romance mentor.

"You know how it happened," he muttered. "A beautiful barista with a killer smile and a sweet Southern accent approached you." One who was still off-limits. One who had no idea he was spying on her for a big fat paycheck.

He felt slightly flattered that Sophie regarded him as an expert, but it couldn't be further from the truth. Noah never had a problem getting dates or attracting women, but his relationships never lasted long. Other than his ill-fated love affair with Kara, he couldn't remember another romance he'd had with any substance.

Although he had agreed to meet up with

Dwight later on, after his shift, Noah wasn't looking forward to it. Dwight seemed like a good guy, but Noah already had his hands full with his work schedule and keeping Sussex apprised of Sophie's comings and goings. What did he really know about romancing women, anyway? If he did, wouldn't he have settled down himself by now?

He held his cell phone up to his ear and listened to his messages. There were six in all from Sussex. Noah winced and held the phone away so he wouldn't suffer damage to his hearing. The man was acting like a toddler having a tantrum. His client was not in a good mood, presumably because he hadn't heard from Noah in several days.

Noah wasn't proud of himself for dodging the calls. For the first time in his life he was avoiding talking to a client. Now that Sophie had caused him to doubt Sussex's version of events, Noah felt even guiltier about this assignment.

He was stuck between a rock and a hard

place. Should he confront Sussex? Without this gig, his life in Seattle would quickly unravel. His company would be toast. And it wouldn't affect just him. He had employees who were counting on him to rescue the company. If he didn't, their lives would be turned upside down, as well. Noah knew he was afraid to fail as a businessman. His own parents had weathered hard financial times, yet they had always managed to keep the diner afloat.

And Sophie. He cringed at the idea of her finding out he'd been hired to report on her every move. What would she think of him? He cared more than he'd like to admit about Sophie's opinion of him.

Sophie Miller was some kind of wonderful. He let out a chuckle at the memory of their first meeting at the café. How could a person ever be ready for a flash of lightning? Was it possible that he'd been hit by a thunderbolt? He now knew exactly why Sussex was so determined to hang on to Sophie

Miller. She was the sun that everything revolved around. She shone brighter than diamonds. He reckoned that she was a force of nature that could move mountains.

Noah could very well see himself falling for the beautiful barista if he wasn't careful. A man would have to be crazy not to see her appeal. He needed to guard his heart.

Under different circumstances, Noah wouldn't hesitate to ask Sophie out on a date. It would be selfish to pursue anything more than friendship with her, even though he knew there was something brewing between them. It wouldn't be fair to Sophie, since she had no idea he was in Love under false pretenses. From the sounds of it, she had already dealt with major betrayals in her life.

It would be easy to sit back and forget the reasons he'd ever set foot in this town. There was something soothing and comforting about the community of Love. Being here made him feel as if he could put aside all his troubles, although with Sussex blowing up his cell phone, that wasn't likely to happen. He served as a constant reminder that Noah was on his payroll and that his presence in Love was strictly business.

After digging himself out of the driveway, Noah headed into town and straight toward his destination—the Free Library of Love. The moment he stepped inside, he began to deeply inhale. He loved libraries. The smell of them. The way the books felt in his hands. The hush of stillness in the air. No sooner had he walked a few paces than he was greeted by the librarian standing behind the main circulation desk.

"Hi there. I'm Annie O'Rourke, head librarian. Is there something I can help you with this morning?" The sweet-faced brunette smiled at him.

"Hi, Annie. I'm Noah Callahan," he replied. He wasn't certain, but he thought her eyes widened upon hearing his name.

"Nice to meet you, Noah," she said in a perky tone.

"Could you point me in the direction of the true-life crime novels?"

"Sure thing." Annie nodded. "Just follow me."

"Are you any relation to Declan O'Rourke, the pilot?" he asked. "He flew me into town when I first arrived."

"I'm proud to say I am." She wagged her ring finger at him. "We're newlyweds. I came to this town to head up the new library and to find adventure. In the end I found my life partner." She grinned at him. "You never know what's around the corner for you here in Love."

"I'm not looking for entanglements," he said in a firm voice. "I came to town for a job. I do love living here, though."

Annie nodded again. "Let me know if you need any additional help. This section right here is full of great choices." She walked away briskly.

Noah hoped he hadn't sounded rude, but he didn't want to give the wrong impression about his presence here in town. As it was, he'd already had a dozen or so invitations to dinner and town events from single women. Although he had been flattered, there wasn't a single one who'd tempted him.

Well, there is one, he reminded himself. A beautiful redhead. But she was the last person he should pursue. Crossing the line with the person you were investigating was a recipe for disaster. Noah wasn't going down that road.

"Mornin', Noah." The greeting came from behind him. He quickly turned around at the sound of Sophie's voice.

For a moment Noah simply allowed himself to soak Sophie up like rays of sunshine streaming down on him on a gorgeous sunny day. "Hey, Sophie. How's it going?" he asked, surprised to see her out of her Moose Café uniform. She was wearing a pretty pink sweater and a dark pair of jeans.

She had a stack of books in her hands. One false move and the books would tumble out of her arms.

He reached over and took them from her. "Let me help you with these. They probably weigh more than you do." Noah placed them on the table next to him.

Sophie seemed content to let him take the books off her hands. "Phew. Thank you. I love coming to the library, but I always end up with more reading material than I can handle. I forgot my tote bag at home. I'm thankful I didn't topple over."

Noah chuckled. There was a look of such earnestness on her face.

"No worries. I would have caught you," he said in a teasing voice. He was actually serious. There was something about Sophie that brought out his protective side.

He looked down at her books. "What do you have here?" He began reading the titles out loud. *Thirty Places to Visit before You Turn Thirty. A Guide to Spotting Alaskan*

Birds. How to Find the Love of Your Life in Six Easy Steps." Noah swung his gaze up to look at her. Clearly, she really was interested in finding love.

"Interesting books." His words were loaded with meaning. As a result, Sophie's cheeks turned rosy.

"You've got quite a few books yourself," she noted, her eyes widening as she scanned the titles. "True crime." She shuddered. "Books like that give me the willies. I wouldn't be able to catch a wink of sleep if I read this type of material."

"Let's just say I'm a bit of a crime buff," Noah admitted. He supposed it was one of the reasons he'd been drawn into the world of private investigations and security. There were a lot of bad guys in the world, and he wanted to be able to figure them out before they hurt innocent people. Suddenly, he felt like the world's biggest hypocrite. Wasn't he potentially harming Sophie by continuing this ruse? If she had been telling the truth it might mean Sussex couldn't be trusted. In that case, shouldn't he warn her? His chest tightened. Doing so would be violating the rules of his profession.

"I guess great minds think alike. Working at the Moose doesn't afford me much library time." Sophie looked around her and let out a sigh of contentment. "This place is divine."

"It's a great place to hang out," Noah said. "I like the quiet. Growing up in a rowdy household made me crave moments of pure silence."

Sophie smiled. "I'm actually the opposite. As an only child I longed for loud noises and the sound of doors slamming and running feet. You have no idea how blessed you are to have so many siblings."

"They're a tough bunch, but for the most part they're keepers," Noah said.

"Thanks again for agreeing to help out with Dwight. He's such a sweetheart. He truly hides his light under a bushel. Most people here in town find him a bit grating, but he's really a very special person." Sophie was in full cheerleader mode.

It sounded like she was trying to sell him on Dwight. Uh-oh. Perhaps he'd misread the situation. Most of the time when the majority of the people in a town didn't care for someone it meant the person had big huge annoying flaws. He prayed it wasn't the case with Dwight, considering the fact that Noah was now mentoring him. Whatever that meant.

"So, I was wondering if you'd like to go with me to the Founder's Day celebration?" Sophie blurted the question out at such rapid speed that he almost asked her to repeat herself. Judging by the near panic etched on her face, he didn't dare. It was a look of such sweet awkwardness and bravado.

If he was using reason and logic, Noah should turn down Sophie's invitation. He needed to keep his eye on the prize and do the work he'd been hired to perform. Getting closer to her was only going to make him more conflicted about this assignment. There were too many people back in Seattle who were counting on him to keep Catalano Security afloat. He didn't need to start second-guessing himself and this profitable gig.

Eyes on the prize, he reminded himself.

Once he saw the hopeful glint in her eyes, Noah didn't have the heart to say no. Truthfully, he didn't want to. Even though he knew it would be like walking on thin ice in springtime, his every instinct was telling him to say yes.

There! She'd done it. Even if Noah said no to her invitation—which would be incredibly awkward and humiliating—Sophie had stepped out on a ledge. No guts, no glory! She wanted her first date in Alaska to be with a man who gave her goose bumps. And that was Noah Callahan. She hadn't even meant to ask him, but the words had just slipped out.

She locked gazes with Noah, resisting the

urge to look away from his intense stare. She felt as if she was holding her breath, waiting for him to answer her. It was nerve-racking.

The corners of his mouth slowly began to lift up into a smile. "Sure thing, Sophie. I'd love to go with you." The deep timbre of his voice made her pulse race with excitement.

Sophie blinked at Noah. She hadn't really expected him to say yes.

"You would?" she asked. "Seriously?" Suddenly it felt as if she had wings and could fly.

"Of course I would. Actually, you're the only woman in town I wanted to ask me. You've been a good friend." He winked at her. "Truthfully, I was thinking about asking *you*."

"Just thinking about it, huh?" she stated, wondering what had stopped him.

A sheepish expression crept over his face. "We work together at the Moose Café. I wasn't sure if it would make things awkward between us."

"I don't think so. It's not like we're dating or anything," Sophie said, making a funny face. "We're pals." Something about her expression caused Noah to burst out laughing. Sophie soon joined in, to the point where they were making way too much noise for library patrons. An older woman with glasses frowned at them.

Suddenly, Annie was standing a few feet away, shushing them with her finger at her lips. Although her expression was slightly stern, Sophie had the impression she was getting a kick out of seeing her with Noah. She caught Annie flashing her a thumbs-up before she walked back toward the circulation desk.

"Has anyone ever given you the ten-cent tour of Love?" Sophie whispered.

"No. I've been poking around ever since I got to town, but I'm sure that I missed some key landmarks."

Sophie took a quick glance at her watch. "We have some time before we have to arrive at work. You could drive while I navigate. I'm game if you are."

"Sounds like a plan," Noah said, scooping up his books and Sophie's from the table. "Let's go."

Sophie checked out her books, then waited as Noah filled out an application for a library card. It gave Sophie a rush to see him doing something so mundane. His life in Love was taking shape piece by piece. It mattered to her whether he stayed in town or if he departed. Since Sophie had been in Love there had been numerous transplants who had changed their minds about living in the wilds of Alaska and returned home. It would be heartbreaking if Noah followed suit and left town.

Sophie didn't want to think about him leaving. And she definitely didn't want to probe why the idea made her so sad. She had no business getting attached to Noah, especially since there were secrets she was harboring about her true identity. She had no illusions about Noah's feelings toward her. He viewed her simply as a friend. There was no sense in hoping for more. Noah seemed like a humble, simple man who happened to resemble a model for *GQ* magazine and could cook like a master chef. He didn't seem like a man who would tolerate any type of deception.

Telling him about John and her estrangement from her father was one thing. Revealing her identity as the Java Giant heiress might change the way he viewed her. Sophie let out a sigh. In her experience, it always did. Sophie's past was littered with people who'd developed their own agendas once they discovered her level of wealth. It had broken her heart time after time. More than anything, Sophie wanted to be viewed as a unique person in her own right. She never wanted to be viewed as an extension of the empire her father had built.

Annie had a very pleased expression on her face as she helped Noah obtain his library card. She kept darting her gaze toward Sophie and making gestures with her eyes and brows. Sophie pretended not to notice, and she hoped Noah hadn't, either. The last thing she wanted was for him to think all her friends were conspiring to pair them up.

"Have a wonderful day, you two," Annie called out after them. "Thanks for visiting the Free Library of Love."

Once they made their way to Noah's vehicle, Sophie settled in the passenger seat while he took the wheel and negotiated the snowy streets of Love. As they drove down Jarvis Street and past the quaint downtown shops, Sophie pointed out all the stores and landmarks.

"That's the local bookstore. It's called The Bookworm and it's a great place to find unique, one-of-a-kind books. And right next door is the pawn shop." Her voice rose with excitement. "Lulu's Beauty Shop just opened up a few months ago. Lulu is a gal who came over to be a part of Operation Love. She did us all a favor and opened a place for hair, nails and eyebrows. Let's just say she's become a local heroine."

As they drove by the Moose Café, Sophie felt a burst of pride. Cameron's establishment was a town favorite. With its wooden sign embossed with gold, Cameron had managed to add a few stately touches to the place. The huge bay window allowed passersby to get a peek at the interior. Normally, there was a soft glow emanating from inside. According to Hazel, it made the customers feel warm and fuzzy about the place.

"Should I keep going straight?" Noah asked, not taking his eyes off the road. Sophie appreciated his diligence. All morning she'd been hearing about icy conditions. When Hazel had dropped her off at the library earlier, her truck had slipped and slid all over the street. Thankfully, Hazel was a great driver who had all-wheel drive and studded tires to help her make it through Alaskan winters.

"I want to show you the building where Hazel's Lovely Boots are made. If you go straight, then take a right on Seaport, it will lead us down to the docks."

Noah followed her instructions, which led them right to Kachemak Bay, where local fishermen docked their vessels and unloaded their hauls after a day spent fishing. It was a picturesque area, where one could gaze out and see nothing but water for miles and miles. Sophie had a tender spot in her heart for this spot. The moment she had stepped out of Declan O'Rourke's seaplane, this had been her first view of the town.

"If you park over here we can take a gander at the building," Sophie said, waving her hand. Noah steered the car into the lot and placed it in Park. Once they got out of the car, the salty smell of the bay drifted toward them, serving as a reminder that one of the town's biggest industries was fish— mainly halibut and salmon. Although stocks weren't as plentiful as in past years, local fishermen still relied on them to make a living. Many fishermen frequented the Moose Café, where Sophie enjoyed hearing their tales of adventures out on the water. They were some of the nicest individuals Sophie had ever met—hardworking and proud.

"This is where we landed when Declan flew me into town on his seaplane," Noah observed, pointing toward the dock. "That landing was as smooth as glass."

"We landed there, as well," Sophie said. "I remember thinking it was going to be the start of a wonderful adventure."

"And has it been?" Noah asked, a curious expression etched on his face.

"More than in my wildest dreams," Sophie said. "I'm gainfully employed at a hip coffee bar, I've made lifelong friends and I've learned to embrace who I am. I spent a long time trying to live up to the expectations of people who didn't seem to value me as a person." In addition to her father and John, there had been numerous friends and acquaintances who had wanted Sophie to be a society princess and spend her life partying with other rich socialites. That lifestyle had never appealed to her and she had rejected it time after time, choosing instead to focus on simple values and her faith.

"I feel comfortable in my own skin for the first time in years," Sophie admitted. Her one hang-up was the secret she'd been harboring.

"It sounds like you've found a real haven here."

A haven. Noah didn't realize it, but his words were right on point. By its very definition a haven was a place of safety or refuge. A sanctuary. She'd found her happy place here in Love. It wasn't perfect by any means, but for the first time in her life Sophie felt free and unfettered. The only thing weighing her down was her estrangement from her father and the secret about being the Java Giant heiress.

"God answered a lot of my prayers by

pointing me toward this town and allowing me to thrive here. I hope you feel that way, too, Noah. Maybe not today or tomorrow, but over time you'll realize that even though you strayed from your faith, God never left your side."

"I do feel blessed. I don't know how to put it into words, but being back in Alaska makes me feel more connected to God and the life I want to live. I feel more grounded. It doesn't seem like such a stretch anymore to believe that He has good things in store for me and that He has always been here, even when I tried to block Him out."

It made her feel good to know Noah's faith was being restored, bit by bit. She didn't want to analyze why it made her so happy. It scared her a little bit knowing Noah was becoming more important to her each and every day. She wondered if he would ever want to get out of the friend zone with her?

Sophie turned away from the water and

faced the building sitting up on the hill. She pointed toward it.

"This building represents hope. A few years ago this town was all set to open up a cannery. It was going to bring new jobs and opportunities to Love. To make a long story short, greed got in the way and the funds were embezzled. The cannery never even opened and this building sat here, unfinished and idle. Fast forward a couple of years and Hazel is making her gorgeous boots and selling them around town. My best friend, Grace, relocated to Love at the same time as I did, and in a moment of pure genius suggested that the town manufacture Hazel's boots as a way to boost revenue. It was Cameron's wife, Paige, who suggested we use the factory for Lovely Boots." Sophie clapped her mittened hands together. "Voilà. The town now has a viable enterprise, and according to Jasper, sales are doing very well."

Noah let out a whistle. "This town really

is extraordinary. Who knew Hazel was such a superhero?"

His comment made Sophie grin. On certain days she felt the very same way about her dear friend.

"I wanted to share that story with you because it shows a lot about the people of Love. They've endured hard times and risen above them using ingenuity and their creative juices. And they always had hope, regardless of their circumstances. They endured. Faith can move mountains. It can restore a struggling town. It can make people hold out for a brighter day."

"I have the feeling you're sending me a message, Sophie." Noah regarded her intensely. "Am I right?"

She nodded. "I am. The other day you mentioned stepping away from your faith. I know what that feels like to be so conflicted. When Mama died I was only a little girl, but I was so angry at God that I stopped believing in Him. I used to sneak outside at night and look up toward the heavens and scream at Him. I blamed Him for Mama dying. It took me a long time but I finally realized I didn't want to walk through life without Him. Because even though there were shadows, there was always plenty of sunshine."

Noah stepped toward her so there was no distance between them. He reached out and palmed her cheek with his hand. "You are living proof of that. I've never known anyone who shines like you do."

Sophie basked in the compliment. "I think that's the sweetest thing anyone has ever said to me, Noah."

He leaned his head down toward her, and Sophie knew without a shadow of a doubt that she was about to be kissed by the dreamiest cook in all of Alaska. Maybe he did want something more than friendship.

All of a sudden, the loud blaring of a horn rang out in the stillness of the morning, jarring them. Noah stepped away from her and swung his gaze back toward Kachemak Bay.

There was a flurry of activity on the pier, with workers rushing toward the site where the boat would dock.

Disappointment washed over Sophie. She had wanted to share a kiss with Noah more than her most heartfelt words could express.

Before Sophie and Noah knew it, twelve o'clock arrived and it was time to begin their shifts at work. Once Noah got into a groove in the kitchen, the time passed by quickly. Thoughts of Sophie made him grin throughout the day. Whenever he caught a glimpse of her in her quirky moose T-shirt, it gave him a reason to smile.

As soon as his shift ended, he headed toward the dining area, where he'd agreed to meet Dwight. This evening an indie band was scheduled to perform at the café as a monthly promotion Cameron had created to draw in more customers. So far the place was still fairly quiet, which meant he wouldn't have to shout over a noisy crowd while they talked.

"Hey, Dwight. How's it going?" Noah asked as he approached his table and sat down. Even though there were a few hundred other things he could be doing right now, he'd promised Sophie to help her friend. Noah wasn't about to break a promise to her, even if watching paint dry sounded better than counseling the town treasurer on his love life.

Dwight frowned. "Fair to middling, I suppose. If you want to know the truth, I'm still hopelessly single and pining away for a woman who didn't even have the decency to say goodbye to me before leaving town. I really thought Marta might be the one." Dwight took a breath, then continued. "If I had muscles, chiseled facial features and a body of an athlete, I'm sure the women in this town would flock to me. But when God was handing out those attributes He must have forgotten all about me."

For a few moments Noah didn't utter a single word. He simply stared at Dwight and counted to twenty in his head.

"First of all, you need to stop with the pity party, Dwight," he said. "It's a huge turnoff."

Dwight sat up straight in his chair and leaned forward across the table. He adjusted his glasses. "Excuse me? What did you just say?"

Noah met his stare head-on. "I said you need to knock off the poor-me routine. In case you haven't noticed, it isn't getting you very far in the love department. As a general rule women don't like men who whine, complain about their lack of good looks or lack self-confidence. The last time I checked, God gifted you with a bunch of attributes, most of which you're not using in your favor."

Dwight sputtered. "Name one."

"You're smart, Dwight. Women love smart men. Not in an arrogant, I-know-it-all way, but in an informative, polished manner. I don't know who you're comparing yourself to, but you're a good-looking guy."

Dwight fiddled with his glasses. "I am?" he asked.

Noah squinted as he studied him. "Honestly, I think you might want to wear a pair of jeans every now and again rather than suits and bow ties. You want to seem relatable. Sometimes you can project a fuddy-duddy vibe."

Dwight was furiously writing down all Noah's comments in a small notebook. He looked up and nodded. "This is good stuff, although I disagree with the fuddy-duddy comment."

All of a sudden Finn O'Rourke made an appearance at their table. The brother of pilot Declan O'Rourke, he had become one of Noah's biggest fans. He came to eat at the Moose Café a few times a week, usually for breakfast. In Noah's opinion, he was just as likable as his brother.

Finn slapped his hand on Noah's shoulder. "Hey, Noah. Dwight. I just came over to give my compliments to the cook." Finn flashed a huge grin at Noah. "That breakfast burrito you made me the other day was the best I've ever had." He rubbed a palm over his stomach. "If I'm not careful I could gain a good twenty pounds eating your meals."

Dwight rolled his eyes and let out an indelicate snort.

"Thanks for the kind words," Noah drawled. "Next time I'll use fat-free ingredients in your breakfast burrito."

Finn chuckled, then said, "Don't you dare."

Once he had walked away, Dwight piped up. "He's a prime example of the stiff competition in this town. Girls fawn over guys like Finn, who has chiseled abs and movie-star good looks. The last time I checked he's not even gainfully employed. He's a bit of a rover."

Noah held his tongue for a moment, reminding himself that it took all kinds of people to make a world. Dwight—bless him—suffered from a serious lack of self-esteem. Noah knew he couldn't cure it, but he could provide him with a dose of common sense.

"First of all, beauty is in the eye of the beholder. One person might think a Picasso is junk, while another hails it as a masterpiece. And I've dated women who were gorgeous on the outside, but mean as a snake on the inside where it matters most. Hating Finn isn't going to bring you any closer to finding your match. It's dwelling on the negative, when you should be focusing on showing yourself in the best light. We all have flaws, but don't lead with that when you're trying to make an impression."

Dwight ducked his head. He didn't speak for a few moments. When he looked up again his eyes were glassy. If he started crying, Noah knew he would throw in the towel and go home. He could take only so much.

"Thanks for the reality check. I do tend to focus on the negative. I always have. And you're right about Finn. He's a pretty nice guy, so I shouldn't pick him apart. I shouldn't be jealous of him or you or any other man in Love. Nobody ever gained anything in this world by focusing on what they don't have."

Relief swept through Noah. Dwight wasn't clueless. He got it. He just needed to get his head out of the sand and take action.

Noah splayed his hands on the table. "So, what I think you should do is focus on a lady you want to ask out on a date. Maybe to the Founder's Day celebration. Then approach her with confidence, not cockiness. Use your wits and charm. And whatever you do, don't fall into self-pity. Even if she says no, keep smiling."

Dwight's face blanched. "You think she'll say no?"

Noah let out a groan. "No, Dwight. I was just throwing that out there as a possible scenario. As I said, stay confident. Don't make it the be-all and end-all of your life."

Noah looked around him. The café had

filled up with patrons. He noticed Sophie sitting at a table with a few other ladies he didn't know. He felt a pang in his heart as he watched her. She was giggling over something and her entire face was lit up with sheer joy. Noah knew he'd never seen such a glow on any other woman's face. It was a reflection of who Sophie was on the inside, he imagined. She radiated from within.

Sophie glanced over at Noah and sent him a little wave. He smiled and nodded at her.

"It seems I'm not the only one looking for love, am I?" Dwight said.

Noah swung his gaze toward him, and found his eyes alight with interest. He had clearly seen Noah staring at Sophie.

Noah shrugged. He wasn't going to deny his interest in her. "I haven't been very successful in the love department, Dwight."

Dwight couldn't contain his surprise. "I would have thought you'd be like catnip for the ladies. Pardon the expression, but you have it all. Good looks. Charm. A nice physique. And in addition to all that, you're a good guy. I really appreciate you taking the time to help me. You must really have it bad for Sophie if you agreed to spend your evening tutoring me."

Noah sighed. Dwight had hit the nail right on the head. He had it bad for Sophie. They had almost kissed earlier. Although the situation was complicated, Noah knew his feelings for her were the real deal. They continued to grow despite his attempts to stuff them down into a dark hole.

He was sick to death of trying so hard not to like someone. Noah liked Sophie. A lot.

"Since coming to Love I've learned to be a little more hopeful," Noah said. "I don't know if love is in my future, but I'm a little more open to it these days."

He pushed his chair away from the table and stood up. He'd put this off for way too long. It was time to contact Sussex and hash some things out.

"See you around, Dwight."

The man stuck out his hand and Noah reached for it. "May we both find what we're looking for," Dwight said with conviction.

"From your lips to God's ears," Noah said as he cast one last look in Sophie's direction before beating a fast path out of the Moose Café.

As he walked out into the frosty night, Noah knew he'd come to a crossroads. Talking to Dwight had been more than a thankless task. Somewhere during their discussion Noah had realized the two of them weren't all that different. He also wanted love in his life. For some time now he'd wanted to change his romantic situation. He had begun to yearn for the things his parents had—a home, security, a partner to have and to hold. And then he had arrived in Love, and despite his initial fears about Sophie, she had nestled her way into his heart.

A heavy weight was sitting on his chest. He felt a little bit breathless. At the present moment he was existing in two different worlds. In one he was working undercover for a client he wasn't quite certain had told him the truth. But his entire life in Seattle depended on Sussex's paycheck. In the other he had found a wonderful Alaskan hamlet with people who trusted and believed in him, even though he was lying to their faces.

And he had found Sophie, a woman who made him feel as if he could accomplish anything he set his mind to if he believed in it hard enough.

Chapter Nine

The day of the Founder's Day celebration had dawned. Sophie had arisen earlier than usual, eager to greet this new day. Grace had come over to help her with her hair and makeup, neither of which were areas of expertise for Sophie. Baby Eva was sleeping comfortably in her carrier nearby, completely oblivious to their chatter. As soon as Grace arrived the conversation had quickly turned to Noah.

"This Noah Callahan must be pretty special," Grace noted. "I haven't seen you this excited since we arrived here in town."

Sophie nodded. "I've gone on plenty of first dates in my life," Sophie acknowledged. "But to be honest, I'm not sure this is anything more than two friends attending an event together. We've developed quite a rapport. He makes me feel things I've never felt before. But I don't think he wants to be more than friends."

Suddenly, Sophie felt bashful. It was so hard to describe her feelings for Noah. Things had shifted between them after the Taste of Love event. They'd bonded. It had given Sophie the courage to ask Noah to be her date to the Founder's Day festivities.

Sophie didn't want to label what she was feeling for Noah, but it thrilled and terrified her at the same time.

Experiencing sparks with Noah felt wonderful, but constantly feeling as if she was sitting on a powder keg was uncomfortable. And it was scary to admit she might be the only one of them who felt an attraction. So far, she had no reason to think Noah viewed her as anything other than a buddy.

"So are the two of you an item or not?" Grace asked. "You still haven't given me a straight answer."

Sophie bit her lip. "I think he just wants to be friends."

Grace grinned. "Sometimes friendship can be a great foundation for romance."

Grace and Sophie locked gazes. They smiled at each other. They had arrived in Love on the same seaplane a little over a year ago. During the plane ride their friendship had been cemented when Sophie had held Grace's hand due to her fear of flying. They'd been as thick as thieves ever since. Her best friend was at the top of her list of things she was thankful for.

"What time is he coming to pick you up?" Grace asked, bending down to move her sleeping daughter's carrier a few feet away.

"I told him to come at five o'clock. My pulse is racing so fast I feel like a high-speed train." Sophie began to fan herself with her hand. When had her nerves crept in? Suddenly she felt as awkward as a teenager on her first date. Her heart sank. This wasn't really an actual date.

"Don't be nervous, Sophie. Try to breathe. Just be yourself," Grace urged. Her blue eyes radiated positivity.

It was somewhat ironic for Grace to utter those exact words. *Just be yourself.* Grace was the only one here in Love who knew Sophie's true identity. And although she didn't like keeping secrets from Boone, she had agreed not to tell anyone. Grace firmly believed that it wasn't her story to tell, even though she was a journalist always in search of a juicy tale.

"Being in Alaska has allowed me to be my truest self," Sophie said. "I've never felt more right within my soul than in the past year."

Her friend smiled. "That's what matters most."

"I still miss my father, but the life I was

living in New York was slowly chipping away at me. And I know being at odds with my family isn't right, but I still haven't figured out how to mend those fences. I love my life here in Alaska and I don't want any interference with what I've built here."

Sophie bit her lip. "I feel as if I'm at a crossroads. I worry about starting something with Noah and then having to tell him the truth about being the Java Giant heiress. He might consider it a huge lie. Let's face it. A small-town cook might be affected by news of that variety." Sophie could hear the agony in her voice. The situation was fraught with tension.

"At some point you have to come to terms with all of that, but not tonight," Grace said in a brisk voice. "Right now you're about to get dolled up. Nothing too glamorous, mind you. We wouldn't want to send shock waves through town, would we?"

Sophie and Grace both chuckled. Love, Alaska, was a wonderful and quaint hamlet, but the townsfolk tended to be old-fashioned and sensible, rather than showy and over-the-top. Sophie wouldn't have it any other way. She liked the town's humble vibe. It was a far cry from debutante balls and galas in New York City.

Grace began to work on Sophie's hair, wielding the flatiron like a pro. When she handed her the mirror to see her reflection, Sophie let out a gasp. Grace had managed to create an elegant hairdo, with some of her long hair hanging down, and the rest swept up in a twist. Her makeup was very natural and subtle.

"Gracie, it's perfect. I look…amazing." She turned toward her best friend. "Can I say that without sounding conceited?"

Grace leaned down and hugged her. "Of course you can. And you're the least arrogant person I've ever known. You're gorgeous, Sophie. Inside and out."

"I'm very thankful for your friendship and wise counsel, Gracie. God sure had a hand in our friendship by putting us on the same seaplane."

"He sure did. I'm going to scoot before Eva wakes up and wants to be held or fed. I'll see you later on at the festivities." Grace peered into the carrier and let out a sigh. Baby Eva was still sleeping as quietly as could be.

Sophie walked them to the door and embraced her friend before parting. Grace shook her finger at her. "Remember, Sophie. You're more than enough just as you are. And anyone who doesn't realize it is plumb crazy."

Sophie went into her bedroom and dissected everything in her closet. She still hadn't decided on an outfit to wear tonight. After much deliberation, she chose a pretty sweater dress the color of oatmeal. She paired it up with dark leggings and her warm, fuzzy Lovely Boots. She looked comfortable and fashionable without appearing as if she'd tried too hard.

At ten minutes to five, Sophie heard a knock. She strode toward her door to open it for Noah. He was standing there looking more gorgeous than a person had a right to be, in a black winter coat with a dark pair of jeans. A nice red scarf hung around his neck, lending him a festive air.

"I know I'm early," he told her with a grin. "I made sure I gave myself extra time in case I got lost." He held out a bouquet of flowers for her. Sophie let out a gasp. She waved him inside her cabin.

"These are stunning. Peonies and baby's breath. How did you know these are my favorite?"

Noah smiled, appearing pleased with himself. "I asked Hazel. She was only too happy to point me in the right direction. If I'm not mistaken I think she fancies herself as a matchmaker."

Sophie shook her head. "I promise you I'm not encouraging her." She went to find a vase, which she filled with water. "Now that she's about to walk down the aisle, Hazel feels it's her duty to see that everyone is paired up."

"Well, they don't call it Operation Love for nothing," Noah drawled. He looked around the cabin. "I like what you've done to the place. All the colors are very cheerful."

"When I first moved it, the atmosphere was on the drab side," Sophie said as she arranged the flowers in the vase. "And that's an understatement. Everything was blah and brown. So I asked Hazel if I could paint the walls eggshell and she agreed. Then I just kept adding pieces with lots of color—reds, purples, oranges, deep blues. I made it my own." Sophie felt a burst of pride as she surveyed the living area. "It made a world of difference."

"It's a lot like you," Noah said. "Bright, sunny and a little bit bold."

A girl could really get used to Noah's flattering words, Sophie realized. "If you don't stop giving me compliments I'm not going to be able to fit my head through that door," she teased. "We should be leaving soon for the festivities."

"I'm raring to go. I've never been to a Founder's Day celebration before."

Sophie winked at him. "Well, then, you have no idea how much fun awaits you."

"Shall we?" Noah asked, holding out his elbow for her.

She grabbed her coat and pulled it on, then gently placed a hat on before looping her arm through Noah's. After all the work Grace had done on her hair, Sophie had no intention of messing it up. Since the majority of events were being held outside, bundling up was crucial. Sophie didn't relish turning into a Popsicle. She took a deep, fortifying breath. Her emotions were all over the place. It felt so nice to be walking arm in arm with Noah. When they reached his car he pulled open the door for her, then waited for her to get situated before he closed it.

You can't train someone to be a gentle-

man. Her father's voice buzzed in her ear. It was one of his favorite sayings. Roger Mattson was a big believer in courtly gestures and men acting like gentlemen. She liked to think he would approve of Noah, although she wasn't certain he would appreciate her dating a cook. Although he'd hailed from humble origins himself, her father had become a bit of a snob when it came down to her potential suitors. That's why he'd been so ecstatic about her relationship with his protégé, John.

Sophie and Noah's arrival at the celebration was met with stares and whispers. Sophie knew the townsfolk were brimming with curiosity about him. Noah was new in town and a bit mysterious, according to some of the residents. Sophie had heard snippets of gossip about him, most of which made her giggle and shake her head. Now that they'd shown up together, she knew their names would be linked for weeks and months to come. She prayed it wouldn't bother Noah too much.

She knew from the life she'd led in New York City that being the subject of gossip wasn't always fun. Thankfully, here in Love it wasn't mean-spirited or vicious.

"I think we're on the tip of everyone's tongues," Sophie said in a loud whisper. "Everyone is staring and flapping their gums."

"Doesn't bother me a bit. They're just staring because we're the best-looking pair here," Noah teased. Sophie liked the way his blue eyes twinkled, and there were little laugh lines at the corners of his eyes as he began to preen.

Sophie burst out laughing. "I like your confidence."

He winked at her. "Never let 'em see you sweat." Noah leaned close and whispered, "Matter of fact, we could really put a show on for them if you want." He reached for her hand and raised it to his lips, pressing a kiss on it. Out of the corner of her eye So-

phie could see some of the townsfolk pointing and saying her name in loud whispers.
Deciding to play along, she batted her lashes
in an exaggerated way and ducked her head.

"Let's move along before I break character and burst out laughing," she finally said,
trying to suppress a giggle.

"Where to? I smell something amazing."
He rubbed his stomach. "It would be nice to
eat someone else's food for a change."

"Why don't we go grab something? I
know this year's theme is clambake, so if
you enjoy lobster, crab and other shellfish,
you're going to be a happy camper. It's all
included in the price of the tickets we pur-
chased when we arrived."

As they made their way toward the food,
Sophie and Noah stopped a few times to
speak with people who crossed their path.
It was amazing how in a year's time she had
come to know almost an entire town. Most
of them she considered friends.

Each and every time they met someone,

Noah gave a hearty, warm greeting. It made Sophie feel all warm and fuzzy inside to see him so well connected to the community.

"You've really come out of your shell," she noted as they continued walking.

"I had a shell?" Noah asked, a dumb-founded expression on his face.

Sophie tried not to laugh. "Yes, you did. You were a little closed off and slightly cranky. But once you got into a groove you began to open up. I'm sure glad you did, and so are all the customers. They really love you coming out to the dining area to meet them, in case you didn't know. You're becoming a regular culinary rock star here."

Noah let out a low whistle. "A culinary rock star. That's high praise, Sophie." He bent over and bowed to her with a flourish. "Thank you kindly. My parents would be very proud." He made a face. "Cooking is a big deal in my family. They wanted me to stay in Homer and help run the restaurant."

"And you didn't want to do that?" Sophie

asked. She could relate to Noah's dilemma. It was always a hard choice which road to take. Granted, her circumstances had been different, but the dilemma had been the same—stay or go.

"Pardon the pun, but there were too many cooks in the kitchen. I respect my parents for what they built and for all their hard work, but I wanted something of my own. Something I created from the ground up. I think being the youngest of five boys made me feel as if I always had something to prove. I guess you could call it ambition."

Sophie admired Noah for his pluck and grit. She knew firsthand how difficult it was to break away from family expectations. Noah could have walked right into a position at an established family business, yet he'd chosen to forge his own path. Truthfully, it didn't surprise her one bit. Noah had character. And even though he was a cook at the Moose Café, who knew where his career might take him? She believed in him. One day Noah might open his own restaurant. Knowing he wasn't taking the easy road made her feel so proud of him.

Ruby and her husband, Liam, approached them from the opposite direction as they walked with their five-year-old son, Aidan. As far as Sophie was concerned, all kids should be as adorable as Aidan. With his curly dark hair and warm brown skin, he was a perfect blend of his parents. Sophie quickly made the introductions. Liam and Noah shook hands, while Ruby gave Noah a welcoming hug.

"Guess what I just did?" Aidan asked, jumping up and down with excitement.

Sophie bent down and kissed his cheek. "I don't know, buddy. Why don't you tell me?" Aidan was Sophie's little pal. He came into the café at least once a week, sometimes twice. He ordered so many reindeer burgers that Sophie had a running joke with him about turning into one.

"I got to pet a Siberian husky dog," Aidan

said, his face lit up with joy. "They're the dogs who run in the Iditarod races."

Noah high-fived the boy. "Whoa. That's pretty cool. They're beautiful, aren't they?"

"We might be getting one," Aidan said, his voice full of unbridled enthusiasm. "My mom trains search-and-rescue dogs."

"That's impressive," Noah said, nodding at Ruby. "Those dogs are mighty heroic, and from what I understand, essential to rescue missions."

"They're invaluable," Ruby concurred. "I'm just in the beginning stages, really. I used to be part of an emergency response team." She looked over at Liam and smiled. "But I had an accident and retired from the job. I'm passionate about search-and-rescue, however, so I'm devoting myself to this endeavor and hoping to make a difference."

Sophie felt so many emotions as she gazed at this beautiful family. They had been through so much, and yet here they stood, happy, healthy and united. God had blessed them in so many ways.

"How many Prescotts live in this town? I'm beginning to lose count," Noah said in a loud whisper.

"Don't bother trying to keep track," Sophie teased. "The Prescott family keeps growing by leaps and bounds."

"Big families are nice. I want one of my own. Six kids at least."

Sophie sputtered. "Six? Your future wife might object to that."

Noah looked at her with a twinkle in his eye. "Who knows? Maybe she'll want seven."

Sophie shook her head and chuckled. Noah really knew how to entertain her. She couldn't remember the last time she'd laughed so hard. It felt nice to laugh with Noah rather than fret about her life being a ticking time bomb. For tonight she wasn't going to worry about the cloud hanging over her head.

They walked on toward the food area with Ruby, Liam and Aidan, then settled down to eat at a table in one of the heated tents. More friends joined them, and before they knew it, their table was overflowing with people.

After they finished dinner, Noah made a beeline to the horse-and-carriage ride. When they had passed by earlier, the line had been daunting. Now, all of a sudden, it was non-existent.

"How about a ride?" he asked with a smile.

"How can I say no to that?" Sophie answered.

Noah jumped up into the carriage, then turned to help her aboard. They bundled up under the blanket, and when his gloved hand reached for hers, she felt safe and warm and protected. Sophie had to remind herself that they were just friends.

Sophie wrinkled her nose. She remembered riding in a horse-drawn carriage with John. It should have been romantic and thrilling as they cantered through Central

Park in the snow. John had complained the entire time about the smell of the horses and the biting cold winter's night. He had ruined everything with his sour attitude. Sophie remembered wondering why he couldn't just be happy for simple blessings.

"Are you warm enough?" Noah asked, pulling the blanket even tighter around her.

"I'm nice and toasty. Thank you for being my date tonight. I've had a lot of fun this evening."

"Thank you for inviting me. Participating in this town celebration has made me feel like I'm part of the community."

"Why, of course you are," Sophie said. "I saw how the townsfolk treated you tonight. You've truly become a native son."

"Something tells me I'm getting extra brownie points for cooking meals for them. The folks in this town sure like to eat."

"Yes, they do, although I think the Moose Café appeals to the townsfolk on a social level, too. People seem to really enjoy gathering at the café and eating breakfast with their best friend or the town sheriff. Even the ones who sit by themselves end up talking to the person sitting at the next table, or asking someone to join them."

"You really love what you do, don't you?"

"I really do. For me it's all about the people. Talking to them. Listening to them. Actually hearing what they have to say. Having them care about me as a person. How my day is going. Do my feet ache from standing all day?"

Noah nodded. "I get it. Frankly, I'm surprised at the way the townsfolk check in on me from time to time. They really seem to care about my well-being."

"It's genuine. I can vouch for that," Sophie said. She looked up at the sky and let out a high-pitched squeal. "Noah! Please. Stop the carriage!"

"Hey! What's wrong, Sophie?" Noah's pulse was racing. He had no idea what had caused her to scream like that.

"Look!" she shouted, pointing up at the velvety sky. "It's a blue moon."

Noah swung his gaze up toward the heavens. Staring back at him was a gorgeous teal-colored moon. He'd never seen one in his entire life.

Noah tapped the driver on the shoulder and asked him to stop the carriage. Once he had, Noah hopped out, then helped Sophie down. The carriage driver moved a discreet distance away from them as they both looked up at the sky.

Noah held her in his arms for a moment, enjoying the sweet perfumed smell of her hair as it wafted under his nose. By the time he let her go he was wishing he could hold her a lot longer.

Sophie craned her neck so she could check out the moon. "It's incredible. And what a gorgeous blue color."

Noah looked up at the moon again, marveling at its brilliance. "These are incredibly rare. They usually happen after a dust storm or a volcanic eruption. Sometimes even a forest fire." He felt mystified. "I think this one is just a random occurrence. Serendipity for us."

"It sure is," Sophie said.

"I know they say the moon is always the same size no matter where you are, but doesn't it seem bigger here in Alaska?" he asked.

Sophie turned toward him, a look of awe on her face. "I thought I was the only one who noticed that," she said.

"I noticed that the first time I ever stepped foot off Alaskan soil. As a kid I remember thinking that God just loved Alaska most of all."

Sophie shook her head. "Spoken like a true Alaskan."

Noah stepped closer, then reached out and took her face between his hands. He looked deeply into her eyes, noticing for the first time the flecks of gold mixed with the green. Tiny freckles were scattered across her cheeks and the bridge of her nose. The tip of her nose and her cheeks were rosy. A sigh slipped past his lips. She was simply beautiful.

"I'm going to kiss you, Sophie," he announced, wanting to give her the opportunity to stop him if she was so inclined. He was praying she wouldn't have a single objection. Noah was giving in to the moment, even though he wasn't certain he should be acting on impulse. He wasn't sure kissing Sophie was the right thing to do, but he'd gone too far to turn back now.

"Yes, please," she murmured. "I'd like that very much."

Noah leaned down and placed his lips on hers. Suddenly, everything grew hushed and still around them. Nothing mattered at this moment but the two of them. Despite the frigid temperature, Sophie's lips were warm and soft. Inviting. They tasted sugary and sweet. He felt her hands reach up to rest on his shoulders, and a honeyed smell rose to his nostrils.

As the kiss ended, Noah rested his forehead against hers. He pressed one last kiss on her forehead before pulling away.

"Wow!" Sophie said, sending him a sweet smile. "As far as kisses go, that was pretty sensational."

Noah chuckled. He loved her honesty. "It was, wasn't it?"

"I haven't been kissed in a very long time," she admitted. She looked at him cautiously, as if she wasn't certain of his response to her statement.

"No? That's a shame, Sophie. Because you are a woman who should be kissed on a regular basis."

Sophie's cheeks were pink. Noah wasn't sure if it was due to the frosty temperature or the kiss they had shared. Or maybe even his comment about her being very kissable.

She stared at him, her brows knitted together. "So why aren't you off the market, Noah? I'm sure women fall all over you."

He thought for a moment about how to answer that loaded question. "I haven't met the one yet, I suppose."

She cocked her head to the side. "So you believe in that?"

Noah shrugged. "I guess so. Maybe. Honestly, I haven't believed in it for quite a while," he admitted.

"Who was she?" Her voice was infused with tenderness.

"She who?"

Sophie gazed at him with a somber expression. "The woman who dented your heart."

Noah didn't even bother denying it. The knowing look on Sophie's face spoke volumes. He'd been carrying Kara's betrayal around with him for so long it was no doubt etched on his face. Lately, though, he had begun to let some of it go.

"Her name was Kara." Just saying her name out loud made Noah feel as if a weight had been lifted from his chest. For so long now he'd hidden Kara away like a dirty little secret. She'd made him feel like a fool, so he'd been ashamed and embarrassed to talk about the pain she'd caused him. Growing up in a family of five boys had taught him to keep his chin up and put on a brave face, even when he was dying on the inside. His father had unknowingly instilled it in his sons to "never let your pain show on the outside," so he had bottled up his feelings and never allowed himself to venture down that path again.

"That's a pretty name. Was she beautiful?" Sophie asked, her emerald-colored eyes gleaming with interest.

Noah nodded. With her dark hair and hazel eyes, Kara had been stunning. "Yes. She was. On the outside. On the inside— not so much. She was very calculating and selfish. And—"

"She broke your heart?" Sophie blurted out the question.

Noah sighed. "Yep. She smashed it into little pieces and went on her merry way. She didn't even look back to see the damage she'd done to me. She was very wealthy. One of those types who was born with a silver spoon in her mouth. I fell hard for her. And she looked down on all of my aspirations." He let out a harsh laugh. "I wasn't good enough for her. She dumped me for a rich guy who could keep her in the lifestyle to which she'd become accustomed."

"Oh, Noah, that's awful."

"I trusted her and she stabbed me in the back in many different ways. I'm a little jaded about love, Sophie. That's why I was skeptical when we first spoke about Operation Love."

"I understand," Sophie said in a soft voice. "When someone hurts us it's very hard to put our hearts out there again."

Noah studied her calm expression. "But you've been hurt by your ex-fiancé and you still believe in happy endings. Maybe I'm just a skeptic."

"If I didn't believe in happy endings it would make the world a lot less bright and joyful," Sophie said.

Noah quirked his mouth. "That's a good way to put it."

"For me, it's belief. I came to Alaska on a leap of faith. During the rough days, God keeps me going. He's invested in me, so I make sure I return the favor."

"You have bad days?" Noah asked with a disbelieving shake of his head. "I never would have guessed. You project such positivity."

"Doesn't everyone have tough times? I just try to put one foot in front of the other and hold fast to the things I know to be true."

"Such as?" Noah asked, wanting to know as much about Sophie as he could. She fascinated him. And it didn't have a single thing to do with his assignment. Sophie made him feel as if he needed to be more like her—full of hope and goodness.

She looked up at the sky full of stars. "I deserve to be happy. And God loves me. At my lowest moments He's there with me. I can't give up on myself, because God never has. And I can't blame Him for the hardships. Everyone has them. No one in this world is immune from pain."

Noah allowed Sophie's profound words to flow through him. He took a moment to absorb the full impact of her message. *God loves me.*

He'd never quite thought about it like that before. Sophie hadn't let her personal disappointments get in the way of her relationship with God. Her faith was still strong. She continued to believe that God was gracing her life.

How many blessings had Noah dismissed in his life? There were so many amazing things that had been bestowed on him. After Kara's betrayal he had shut himself off from love, yet he'd also stepped away from his faith. If he was being honest with himself, he'd admit that he had blamed God for the pain and heartache, when in reality it had boiled down to Kara's poor character and his being blinded by love.

Noah let out a hollow laugh. "Sophie, not only are you beautiful and kind, but you're wise and insightful. You've reminded me of something important." He shook his head. "A very precious thing I lost sight of when life became difficult. I doubted myself and then I began to question God. I did the very opposite of what you did."

She reached out with her mittened hand and squeezed his. "We all take our eyes off the prize at one time or another, Noah. The really important thing is making sure we get back on track."

A cold breeze swept past them just then and Sophie shivered.

"We should head back to the carriage before you turn into a polar bear." Noah took her hand and led her back to where the driver was waiting for them.

They spent the remainder of the evening socializing with the townsfolk, enjoying the games and novelties, singing karaoke and eating Hazel's legendary apple pie.

The grand finale occurred when fireworks began to go off over Kachemak Bay. The sights and the sounds highlighted the festive nature of the celebration. Noah felt like a kid again as he gazed up at a sky bursting with all the colors of the rainbow.

As he drove Sophie back to the Black Bear Cabins, he struggled to find all of the words pressing on his heart. As he pulled up in front of her cabin, he sat still for a moment in the driver's seat, wanting to say something meaningful before they parted.

"I'm thankful for this evening," Noah said. "I can't remember the last time I laughed so much or had such a fun time." His heart was full almost to overflowing with gratitude.

Not just toward Sophie, but to God for allowing him to experience such joy.

Noah didn't think he could fully articulate to Sophie what tonight had meant to him. He would probably just trip over the words and make a fool of himself. The feelings she was dredging up inside him were powerful and strong. The town of Love and its residents had wormed their way inside his heart, until now he couldn't imagine not being a part of this wonderful fishing village.

But in so many ways this was all wrong. He was betraying Sophie by working with Sussex to keep tabs on her. He was kidding himself to think anything real could develop between them when secrets stood between them. He imagined the townsfolk would run him out of town on a rail if they knew the reason he'd come to Love.

Noah stuffed those doubts down. For this moment, he wasn't going to focus on them. There would be plenty of time later to deal with the reality of his situation.

He dipped his head and placed a tender kiss on her lips. The kiss was full of everything Sophie had made him feel tonight— hope, an abundance of joy and a renewal of his faith. Noah wouldn't have minded one bit if the kiss had gone on until the stars were stamped out of the velvety Alaskan sky. He felt incredibly connected to her at this moment. He couldn't remember ever feeling this way, as if he was relating to someone on an entirely different level.

He helped Sophie out of the car, then slowly walked her up to her front door. He knew he was trying to stretch out the minutes so this night would never end. Sophie seemed to sense it, too. The smile she graced him with made his heart soar. She reached up and kissed him lightly on the lips before saying good-night and letting herself into her cabin. Noah stood on her porch steps for a few minutes, watching as a light came on until he knew she was safely ensconced in her abode.

He felt at home here in Love, and being with Sophie felt like a Sunday walk in the park. It was nice and comfortable. They were like two pieces of a jigsaw puzzle that fit together.

As Noah drove away from the Black Bear Cabins he found himself wondering about the future. Tonight he'd kissed Sophie. And he had done so only because he wasn't entirely sure his client was being truthful. It hadn't felt like a betrayal to Sussex because Noah now knew from Sophie's own lips that her ex had caused her a world of pain. In life there were always two sides to every story. Or was he just trying to make himself feel better for his actions?

Kissing her had been wonderful, but now, as he looked at it from a distance, he felt overcome with guilt. Sophie had no idea who he really was. He imagined she wouldn't have kissed him if she knew he was a PI sent to Love to watch her. Most likely she would have slapped him in the face. She didn't deserve to be investigated or spied upon. Shame rose up in Noah at the thought that he was now caught squarely in the middle between his feelings for Sophie and his job as a private investigator.

Noah's life goal was to grow each and every day in his pursuit of becoming a better man. Lying to Sophie just might disqualify him. And although their kiss had been perfection, it felt tainted by his lies. He didn't even want to imagine how bad Sophie would feel if she discovered he was working for her ex. Every word coming out of his mouth was tantamount to a lie.

Part of becoming a better man meant dealing with things head-on instead of biding his time. He needed to complete the assignment, collect his paycheck and move on from Love, Alaska. He didn't want to hurt Sophie, but getting close to her while being here in Love under false pretenses was wrong. He knew it all the way down to his soul.

Now, he just had to figure a way out of this tangled web he'd woven.

Due to the four-hour time difference, it wasn't an easy task to talk to Sussex on the phone. But Noah knew there was no time like the present. He wanted this situation dealt with, once and for all. Maybe then he could breathe without feeling a slight hitch in the region of his heart. He was tired of walking on eggshells and feeling conflicted. To continue with the assignment and accept the second portion of his fee would be immoral.

Sussex answered on the second ring. "Catalano. I've been trying to reach you for days. I was beginning to think you were avoiding me." Clearly, his client had recognized his number by caller ID.

"Sorry about that. The time difference has been an issue." Not to mention the fact that he really hadn't wanted to talk to his client at all. At this point he felt horrible discussing Sophie with the man.

"Anything new to report?" Sussex barked.

"Her days are pretty much the same. Working at the Moose Café. The occasional outing with friends. Town events. Nothing of any note."

"Anything on the romantic front?" Suddenly, there was tension in his client's voice.

"No," Noah answered. "She hasn't been out with anyone from the Operation Love program, although plenty have asked."

He could hear a sigh of relief on the other end of the call. It frustrated him. He wasn't going to tell Sussex that Sophie was looking for love in Alaska. That was her personal business, as far as Noah was concerned.

"I did go out with Sophie. We went to a town event together," Noah confessed.

"That's great, Catalano," Sussex said in a robust voice. "I'm happy to hear it."

"I'm confused about something. Sophie mentioned an ex-fiancé, who she discovered wasn't in love with her. She said this man betrayed her. Was it you?" he asked. "Because I don't recall you telling me anything resembling that when you hired me."

The words hung in the air for a moment with no response from his client. Noah could only imagine he was shocked by the direct question. Wealthy types like Sussex didn't like to have to answer to their employees.

"Excuse me, Catalano, but your questions are out of line. You're in my employ, not the other way around," Sussex barked.

"Truth is important in an investigation," Noah said, keeping his voice way more calm than he felt. "Is there anything you'd like to tell me?"

"No. Nothing has changed. I'm planning to get my fiancée back." His tone was frosty.

"Do you think that's realistic? She's built an amazing life for herself in Love." The words slipped out of Noah's mouth, but he didn't regret them.

"I'm not sure why you're questioning my

motives, Catalano. The last time I checked I'm paying you to perform a service. If that's become too difficult for you, I can assure you that I can find other PIs who will gladly take my money. My objectives should be your objectives. Unless, of course, you're no longer interested in salvaging your company."

Noah shouldn't have been shocked by Sussex's thinly veiled threat, but he was. Clearly, his client had done a little digging of his own into Catalano Security. He knew Noah needed a paycheck in order to keep his company afloat, and was using that fact as leverage so Noah would do his bidding. Alarm bells were ringing. This whole thing seemed to revolve around control. Not only of Noah, but of Sophie, as well. Noah didn't like it one bit.

"I'm always working in the best interests of my clients," Noah said.

"Good to know, Catalano. I would hate to think you had aligned yourself with Sophie rather than the man who's employing you." The line went dead just as Noah was about to respond.

Noah felt a chill sweep across his back. Something about Sussex's tone had sounded fairly ominous. He was a man who obviously liked getting his way, not only in life but in matters of the heart. Sussex didn't seem like the sort who would take defeat lying down. Clearly, he hadn't accepted Sophie's decision to walk away from their relationship, but Noah sensed there was way more going on than Sussex was revealing.

All his instincts were telling Noah that this was about way more than an ex-fiancé trying to get his beloved back. The man seemed almost desperate. And sadly, it didn't seem to have a single thing to do with love.

Chapter Ten

Sophie woke up to a beautiful Alaskan morning. She padded to her front door and flung it wide, then stepped out into the cold. After looking up at the sky—it was the color of a robin's egg—she spread her arms as far as she could. She knew it wasn't possible, but she wanted to embrace the day. She was still dressed in her pajamas, flannel robe and fuzzy cat slippers.

"Happy Birthday to me!" she shouted, feeling a little thrill at celebrating her twenty-eighth birthday in a remote fishing village in Alaska. A year ago she never would have imagined the twists and turns her life would take. This, she realized, was her reward for stepping out on a ledge of faith.

Today was the day she stood to inherit half of the Java Giant empire. Strangely, the realization didn't make her feel happy. Her heart did ache due to missing her father. With every day that passed, Sophie realized more and more how she needed to make amends with him. It didn't mean she was going back to her life in New York City, but it would mean reconciliation and forgiveness.

The last few weeks had been wonderful. Sophie knew she was falling for Noah, and it felt like the greatest thrill ride of her life.

"Thank you, Lord, for blessing me with another year of life. I promise to make this my best year yet."

Sophie went back inside and began preparing her breakfast. Cameron had told her not to even think about coming into work this morning until after ten o'clock, so she could be a lady of leisure. It felt luxurious to sit around in her pajamas, watching television and drinking a hot cup of coffee. Feeling celebratory, Sophie added extra sugar and cream.

"Why not?" she asked as she stirred her coffee, her voice ringing out in the stillness of her cabin. "It's my birthday!" She let out a squeal.

Lucy, one of her friends from the gym, swung by and picked her up a little later. Lucy also lived at the Black Bear Cabins, and worked in town at the bookstore. The whole way into town she grilled Sophie about Noah, asking a million questions about their relationship.

"That Noah sure is dreamy," Lucy said with a sigh. "Is he officially your boyfriend?"

"Umm…no. So far we're really just friends," Sophie stated, not wanting gossip about them to spread any further around town. Although she loved Lucy to pieces, Sophie knew her friend liked to run her mouth. And she felt guilty about being involved with Noah when he had no idea about her true identity. Noah was a solid, working-class man who might have very strong opinions about her being a wealthy heiress.

"You two sure would make a great-looking couple," Lucy said, casting a quick glance at her.

The compliment made Sophie feel great, but she knew a relationship was about more than looks and easy charm. Not that she knew anything about a lasting one, but she believed there were certain principles tying couples together.

Faith. If a man didn't love the Lord, Sophie knew she didn't belong with him. God wasn't something she wavered on. And even though Noah's faith had been challenged, he still believed. He still loved God and was working toward mending his shaken faith.

But he had to be willing and able to love her with all his heart and soul and mind.

And he would have to care about her for the woman she was today and accept the fact that she would never live the life of an heiress. She was simply Sophie the barista.

Any man she might fall in love with had to walk in truth. He couldn't betray her or lie to her face or harbor harmful secrets. Sophie knew this was a tough one, considering no one in Love knew her real identity. She wondered if she was giving herself a slight pass, since she truly felt as if her secret wasn't hurting anybody.

Or maybe she was just telling herself it wasn't. How could a lie be innocent?

Sophie truly believed Noah had all the attributes she was looking for, plus many more. Perhaps it was a sign of healing to believe so strongly in him. She wasn't in the same place as she'd been a year ago. She was blooming like a rose in springtime.

Being in Love had served as a panacea for all her hurts. Working at the Moose Café had given Sophie a purpose. It had allowed her to develop friendships with Cameron and Hazel. And Jasper had become her best customer and honorary grandfather.

When they reached the Moose Café, Lucy decided to come inside with her so she could order a white chocolate hot chocolate and a blueberry muffin. As soon as they stepped inside the café, pandemonium broke loose.

"Happy Birthday, Sophie!" Cameron, Hazel and Noah stood by the entrance and shouted at her as she walked in the door. Jasper stood a few feet away holding a bouquet of balloons. A beautiful banner hung above the entrance to the kitchen, announcing her special day. Colorful and festive and cheerful, it made Sophie want to cry with gratitude.

All the customers present began to clap and call her name. Warmth filled Sophie's insides at the many greetings being sent her way. Tears pricked her eyes, but she didn't even try to hide her emotion.

"You guys are the best," she said, looking around at the beaming faces. She locked gazes with Noah and sent him a sweet smile. He grinned back at her, showcasing his perfect set of dimples. The adorable expression on his face made her want to walk right up to him and kiss him.

"Time to get to work," Sophie said, after walking the gauntlet of well-wishers.

Jasper pulled her into his arms and placed a kiss on her forehead. "Happy Birthday, Sophie." He pushed a box tied with a ribbon into her hands.

"Oh, Jasper. You shouldn't have," she exclaimed.

"Well, then, I'll take it back," he retorted, playfully reaching out and tugging at the gift.

Sophie lightly tapped his hand. "Oh, no, you don't. I can't wait to see what's inside." She ripped open the wrapping paper and tugged off the lid of the box. Inside was a necklace with her name, fashioned in crystals, twinkling back at her.

"Jasper! I know I said you shouldn't have, but I'm really glad you did." She threw her arms around his neck and squeezed him tightly.

He patted her on the back. "Anything for you, darlin'. You better let go of me so I can make my way to town hall. If I don't show my face over there they may hold a special election to remove me."

Sophie threw back her head and laughed. "This town would be lost without you, Jasper. Thanks again for the gift."

The rest of her day went by quickly, with many a friendly face popping in to wish her a happy birthday. At three o'clock Sophie's shift was over. She couldn't wait to go home and take a soothing bath before coming back to the Moose Café for her birthday celebration. Hazel and Cameron had joined forces and were throwing her a small shindig. Hazel had been reminding her about it all day.

"Don't forget we're meeting back here

tonight at seven o'clock for your birthday party," she said yet again, wagging a finger at her. "Don't worry, it's not a huge celebration. Just about half the town," she teased.

Sophie wouldn't be a bit surprised if Hazel was telling the truth. Celebrations in the community seemed to multiply in a mysterious way. A dinner party for ten mushroomed into thirty. People sure did enjoy spreading the love, which was one of the reasons she adored this welcoming town.

"Hey, Sophie. Can I grab you for a minute?" Noah asked, coming up behind her as she left the break room with her belongings. If she hurried to the bookstore, she could catch a ride back to the cabins with Lucy.

"Sure thing," she said with a nod. "I'm hitching a ride home with Lucy so I have to be quick or I'll miss out."

"No worries. I'll take you," Noah said. He grabbed her by the hand and led her through the kitchen and out the back door.

He stopped in front of his car, which was

parked a few feet away in the lot. "Happy Birthday, Sophie. Your chariot awaits." Noah waved toward the vehicle.

"Are we going somewhere?" she asked. Her heart began to pound in her chest. Was Noah taking her out for her birthday? Was that why he said he would take her home?

"Yes. We're hitting the open road." Noah's grin was infectious. "I'm giving you a driving lesson."

"A driving lesson?" Sophie's mouth hung open. Her eyes had a glazed expression.

Oh, no! Had he miscalculated? Was it possible he'd misread Sophie and what he'd perceived as her desire to learn to drive? Perhaps this little surprise of his was a big old bust. He'd wanted to do something meaningful for her birthday.

Sophie rushed at him, throwing her arms around him and giving him the tightest bear hug of his entire life. When she finally let him go, her beatific smile made him feel a bit loopy. "I can't believe it! It's the most thoughtful gift ever. It's as if you looked deep down inside of me and saw my heart's desire."

Whoa! He really had hit the nail on the head. "I'm happy I picked the right gift."

"It's just perfect." Sophie's face seemed to be lit up from inside. If someone had asked him, Noah wouldn't have been able to put into words the way he felt at this moment. The intensity scared him. To be able to make Sophie happy gave him a blissful feeling, as if he was walking on air. And he didn't want anything to bring him down from this euphoric high.

For the next hour and a half, Noah gave Sophie her very first driving lesson. He showed her the inner workings of the vehicle—the clutch, accelerator and brake. He taught her how to start the car and how to put it in Park. Noah also demonstrated the way to hold her hands on the steering wheel, how to adjust her mirrors and signal, and lectured her on the importance of wearing a seat belt at all times.

By the time the lesson was over, he felt confident that Sophie was a serious, attentive driving student. With a few more lessons and some road time, she would get her license in no time flat, he was certain.

"If I had to grade you, I'd give you an A plus. You really paid attention to my instructions and you didn't let your nerves get the best of you." It hadn't escaped Noah's notice the way Sophie's hands were trembling at the beginning of the lesson. By the end, she appeared relaxed and confident.

"Thank you, Noah. I can't tell you how good it felt to be behind the wheel on the open road," Sophie said. She leaned over and pressed a kiss on his lips, one that lingered as he allowed her to take the lead. She let out a sigh as the kiss ended.

"If that's the thanks I get, I'll have to give you more driving lessons," Noah said in a joking manner.

"I feel so accomplished," she exclaimed, clapping her hands together. "I love receiving a gift that doesn't have a monetary value. It's priceless."

"Just like you, Sophie," Noah murmured, reaching out and grazing his fingertip over her ruby lips. "Coming here to Love wouldn't have been the same if I hadn't met you."

"I feel the same way. Before you arrived I hadn't really met anyone I fancied," Sophie confessed in a low voice.

"Are you saying you fancy me, Sophie Miller?" he asked, hoping his words didn't make her feel self-conscious. He knew Sophie felt something for him, but he wanted some sort of affirmation from her lips. Surely what he felt for her wasn't one-sided? And if it was reciprocated, Noah knew he would come clean with her and tell her the truth about his PI assignment from Sussex, as well as his real identity. He would move heaven and earth to convince her that his motives had been well-intentioned.

She locked gazes with him. "In case you hadn't already guessed, yes. I fancy you very much."

Just hearing her confirm his hunch made Noah feel like a high-flying kite soaring up in the sky. She had feelings for him. And if he wasn't mistaken, they were deep ones. He was the first man she'd had feelings for since arriving in Love.

He cleared his throat. Noah had been wondering about where Sophie was in the healing process. It was hard to get over being betrayed by someone, especially one you'd been engaged to marry.

His own feelings wouldn't let him stay silent. "There's something I wanted to ask you the other night, but I didn't want to overstep."

Sophie looked alarmed for a moment, then nodded. "Go ahead. Ask me."

"Your ex-fiancé hurt you very badly. Have

you found a way to move past it?" Noah's chest felt as tight as a drum. His heart was thumping wildly as he awaited her answer. He knew what it felt like to walk around with a heart that had been shredded. Kara's treatment of him had left him with a shattered soul. And for the first time in years, Noah felt free of the shackles Kara had placed on his heart.

"I can say with one hundred percent certainty that I'm in a much better place these days. I don't feel as wounded by it. I guess you could say I'm moving toward closure. Sadly, I don't think I ever truly loved John. He was very close to my father, so it was almost a foregone conclusion we would be an item. He pursued me in a rather relentless fashion. When I accepted his proposal of marriage it was for all the wrong reasons. I admit that. But I never sought to use him or diminish him as a human being. I was just young and impressionable and under a lot of pressure. And I foolishly believed I would grow to love him through our union." She let out a sigh. "Coming here was a big wake-up call. I realize now that there's only one reason to marry someone. Love."

Noah heaved a great sigh of relief. It mattered to him whether Sophie was ready and able to build something with him. As a man who cared deeply for her, he'd needed to know the answer to that question. It made Noah feel more grounded in his own relationship with Sophie, and what might be possible for them down the road. Hearing her talk about Sussex had convinced him that she was the wronged party in the relationship. Sussex had fed him a pack of lies.

He knew his grin must be stretching from ear to ear. "I have to admit, I'm happy to hear that."

"Why?" Sophie's simple question, asked with such sincerity, humbled him. She was so innocent and trusting. So genuine.

"Because I care about you very much," he

whispered, running his finger over the slope of her cheek.

He'd been tempted to tell her he had feelings for her, but he needed to come clean with her about being a private investigator before he professed his love. It wouldn't be right to lay that on the table when a lie stood between them. And he might be dragging his feet, but he couldn't bear the thought of upsetting Sophie on her special day.

Birthdays were sacred. Tomorrow he would tell her the truth, when everything had died down and he could break it to her gently, in a quiet setting. Until then he would show her in word and deed how deeply he cared about her. Maybe it would soften the blow that was coming. Noah knew Sophie might never forgive him for his betrayal, but he prayed she would find a way to understand. They both cared about each other in a deep and meaningful way. Surely that had to count for something in the grand scheme of things.

Noah dipped his head and pressed his lips against Sophie's in a tender, celebratory kiss. He wrapped his arms around her waist and pulled her closer. He knew his heart was pounding like a jackhammer. He wondered if Sophie heard it thumping, and if so, did she know it was because of her?

A feeling of dread gripped him. Before he started fantasizing about the future he needed to get control of the present. He needed to speak plainly to Sophie and reveal everything he'd been keeping close to the vest ever since he stepped foot in Love. Just the thought of doing so made his palms moisten.

As Noah drove Sophie back to the Moose Café for her birthday celebration, he battled a serious case of nerves. He had unexpectedly found happiness in this small Alaskan hamlet with the woman of his dreams. He didn't know what he would do if it was all snatched away from him.

Once the party was in full force, Noah got

into the swing of things and focused on celebrating Sophie's special day.

Noah joined in with the others as they sang to Sophie and presented her with a chocolate layered birthday cake, and he found himself wishing for things he'd stopping hoping for ages ago. A woman to have and to hold. Children to teach and nurture. A home where love would be on display in abundance.

He watched as Sophie closed her eyes and blew out the candles on her cake. Noah hoped all her wishes would come true.

Dear Lord. I haven't been one to believe in happily-ever-after, but lately I've changed my tune. Because of Sophie. She's changed me. Her unwavering faith and goodness has transformed me. Please continue to walk on this path with me. I need You now more than ever. Let Sophie hear the truth and see an even greater truth. Can you show her that my love for her far outweighs the things I've kept from her?

He had fallen for Sophie. Noah had tumbled over the edge to a place where there was no safety net. He had resisted the pull in Sophie's direction, but in the end, his feelings had been stronger than his doubts and fears. And it was far too late to reel his emotions back in. But because his feelings were so strong for Sophie, he needed to be completely honest with her. He couldn't go on like this.

There was no question about his next step. He was going to tell Sophie all of his truths. Noah was going to confess everything to her about his profession and his association with her ex-fiancé. And he was going to pray and hope for forgiveness and a new slate here in Love. He would have to come clean with Cameron, also, and figure out a replacement for himself at the Moose Café. And somehow, maybe there was still a shot at salvaging his company. He'd received a huge chunk of payment from Sussex, and by all rights his client owed him the remainder.

Noah was still fighting for Catalano Security and all his employees.

God could move mountains. Sophie had helped restore Noah's faith. She'd shown him that God wasn't done with him yet. She had nudged her way into his heart, until now he wasn't sure if he was coming or going. Surely He could help Noah figure out how to get himself out of this messy situation.

Chapter Eleven

Noah had tossed and turned all night, filled with the knowledge that he might very well lose Sophie today when he told her the real reason he had come to Love, Alaska. He winced at the thought of giving her even one ounce of pain. He shook his head. Maybe he was in too far to come out of this mess in one piece. He hadn't even been truthful about his last name. So many lies stood between them. For a man who never felt afraid, he was quaking in his boots.

Although he wasn't certain the timing was right, Noah knew he had to come clean today. It wasn't right to hold Sophie in his arms and kiss her while sitting on a mountain of secrets. She deserved to know about Sussex and Noah's true profession.

Tonight was Jasper and Hazel's rehearsal dinner. It was a huge event, scheduled one week before the nuptials. They had invited the entire town of Love to enjoy the prewedding festivities. In seven days' time they would be joined as husband and wife. Since the Moose Café wasn't big enough to hold the whole community, they had decided to host the party at the town hall. As mayor, Jasper was able to green-light the celebration.

Noah didn't know a whole lot about weddings, but he did recognize the absolute joy on Hazel's face as her wedding day drew closer.

Noah and Sophie were attending the dinner together. He almost couldn't believe what had transpired over the course of the last month. He'd fallen for the woman he'd been hired to spy on. Never in a million years would Noah have imagined a case of his taking a turn like this one.

He didn't know if he had a future with Sophie. Not until he fessed up to her, and she forgave him. He'd almost told her a dozen times or more. In the end, his cold feet always stopped him in his tracks. For a man who normally feared nothing, the thought of losing Sophie scared him to death.

Now, he was in the middle of a raucous wedding-rehearsal dinner in an Alaskan fishing village. And there wasn't a place he'd rather be than at Sophie's side. She looked all kinds of gorgeous in a long, cream-colored dress and matching heels.

He leaned down and spoke softly in her ear. "When everything quiets down, I want to talk to you about something, away from the hustle and bustle."

"You won't hear any argument from me," Sophie murmured, as he grazed his lips against her temple. It was time. Time to speak plainly and from the heart. He couldn't go on like this any longer.

Noah had practiced his speech to Sophie for hours last night. He would tell her the plain, unvarnished truth. He wouldn't hold back a single detail. And he wouldn't paint himself as an innocent victim, either. He would tell her about the financial troubles with Catalano Security and how desperation had blinded him.

He would wear his heart on his sleeve in the hopes of Sophie understanding his situation and how trapped he'd become.

When the music started playing, everyone headed toward the dance floor. Even Noah began to tap his foot to the upbeat tempo.

Sophie held out her hand. "Care to dance? Or do you have two left feet?" Her eyes danced with merriment.

"Those are fighting words. I'm a great dancer." Noah took her hand and led her to the edge of the dance floor, where it wasn't as crowded. He gracefully twirled her around and executed a few tricky moves he'd learned along the way. Then he pulled her close to him, steering her expertly across the room as they danced up a storm. When the music died down and people exited the dance floor, he led Sophie back to their table.

Suddenly, Noah felt a tap on his shoulder. He turned around, shock roaring through him at the sight of the man standing beside him.

"I can take it from here, Catalano."

Noah froze. It couldn't be. But yet it was. He instantly recognized the polished masculine voice with the slight British accent.

It was Sussex! He was standing two feet away from them, with a smug smile on his face. Noah sucked in a breath to steady himself. What was his client doing here?

Sophie gazed at Sussex with a look of shock and dismay etched on her features. After a few seconds she shifted her gaze back to Noah, confusion radiating from her eyes. She shook her head, clearly in disbelief at her ex-fiancé showing up in this remote Alaskan town, but even more stunned by the fact that he seemed to know Noah.

"How do you know him, Noah? Why is he calling you Catalano?" she asked, skewering Noah to the spot with her eyes.

"Sophie, I—" he began. He couldn't think of a single thing to say to explain it all to her.

"Have you been lying to me about your name?" she asked.

He let out a sigh. "Yes. My real name is Noah Catalano."

His stomach twisted into knots when Sophie winced. A pained expression crept over her face.

"Can we talk in private?" Noah asked, desperate to tell her everything.

Sophie looked around her. People were beginning to openly stare and whisper. She held up her hand, then looked back and forth between the two men. "Let's take this to the main foyer. I don't want to ruin Jasper and Hazel's evening by creating a scene." She turned on her heel and made her way out of the room. Noah followed, ignoring the impulse to stuff Sussex in an empty broom closet.

Once they arrived at the foyer, Sophie didn't waste any time getting down to business.

She turned to face Sussex. "I want the truth, John. How do you know Noah?"

"He's in my employ," Sussex said. "I hired him to keep an eye on you, Sophie. He's a private investigator."

Sophie gasped. Her eyes widened. Her face crumpled. "Noah! Is that true?"

The satisfied expression on Sussex's face didn't escape Noah's attention. He looked like the cat who'd swallowed the cream. He was clearly enjoying exposing Noah to Sophie.

Noah gritted his teeth. His moment of reckoning had arrived. It didn't matter that he'd planned to tell her the truth later today. Almost didn't count. "Yes, Sophie. It's true. But—"

"I can't believe this! You're just as deceitful as John was." She took two steps backward. "I trusted you. You made me believe you were someone I could love and trust and admire!" She raised her hand to her mouth and let out a sob. "You're a private investigator? This whole time you've been paid to spy on me?" She glared at her ex-fiancé. "For him!"

"Not just spy, Sophie," Sussex interjected. "Part of his assignment was to distract you from the other males here in town. A decoy of sorts. That's how much I adore you. I couldn't bear the thought of you being paired up with someone in this rinky-dink town."

"Shut up, Sussex. That's a lie." Noah looked at Sophie, begging her with his eyes to believe him. "He asked me to romance you, but I would never have done that as part of the assignment."

"Isn't that exactly what you did, though? You courted me, flirted with me, told me you had feelings for me. You made me dream of a future with you. The white picket fence covered with icicles and a houseful of kids with runny noses and big blue eyes." She pounded his chest with her fists. "You made me fall in love with you."

"You're in love with me?" Noah asked. Joy flooded through him. For a single moment he reveled in this feeling of pure satisfaction. Sophie loved him back!

"You fell in love with him?" Sussex said in a sneering tone.

"Be quiet, Sussex. I'm warning you," Noah growled. If Sophie loved him, then surely she would hear him out and give him the opportunity to make amends.

Noah swung his gaze toward Sophie. He felt like an absolute idiot. He should have told her the truth a long time ago. Sussex had come to Love not only to win her back, but to expose Noah, who had inadvertently tipped him off by asking pointed questions about the assignment.

Sussex took a step toward Sophie. "My feelings for you haven't changed one iota,

Sophie. You're the love of my life. I still wish to become your husband. I've been waiting patiently for you to realize we were meant to be together," he said.

Noah rolled his eyes. He prayed Sophie wasn't falling for this ridiculous act. The man loved no one but himself. Of that Noah felt certain.

Sophie scoffed. "You don't love me, John. You used me for my father's connections and his vast fortune. You weaseled your way to the top of his corporation. But that wasn't enough, was it? You wanted the heiress, too. Because that way you'd have your entire future wrapped up with a nice little bow. The world would be your oyster."

Heiress? Fortune? Noah's head was spinning. Sophie was wealthy?

"That's not true," Sussex declared.

Sophie let out a harsh laugh. "And something tells me that's why you're here right now. According to my father's grand plan, I inherited half of the corporation on my birthday. You just can't bear the thought of letting everything slip through your fingers, can you?"

"You can't honestly believe that! I'm devoted to you," John cried, appearing wounded. Noah wanted to give him an Oscar for best actor. There were even tears in his eyes.

"I do believe it, John. There's no question about it! So you see, the joke is on you. You hired Noah to spy on me, but it was really a waste of time. I don't want you in my life. I will never marry you! You will never get your hands on my shares of the company."

John's expression hardened. The wheels seemed to be turning in his head. Noah sensed he knew things weren't going his way.

A loud noise rumbled from outside. It was getting louder and louder by the second. People began to spill from the reception room into the foyer. The sound was emanating from the sky.

Aidan came running toward them. "Come outside. It's a helicopter. And it's getting lower and lower to the ground."

Liam peeked out the window. "You're right, son. Pretty cool, huh?"

"Let's go get a closer look," Aidan pleaded, tugging his father by the hand.

At the news of a helicopter landing at Love's town hall, all the guests made their way outside, with the exception of a few stragglers.

Noah didn't take his eyes off Sophie as they joined the crowd. He still needed to clear the air with her. This helicopter was serving as a distraction. Judging by the beleaguered expression on Sophie's face, she had already heard an earful.

"What in the world is going on? Helicopters need clearance before they set down." Jasper angrily shook his fist in the air. "What kind of stunt is this?"

"Maybe it's a special guest for our rehearsal dinner," Hazel suggested. She made a squealing sound. "Perhaps it's one of those Hollywood action stars!"

"I don't care who it is," Jasper grumbled. "I'm the mayor of this town and I didn't receive a single call, email or tweet about this."

The thought of Jasper tweeting provided a slight dose of levity to an otherwise anxious situation. Noah felt an impulse to grab Sophie by the hand and take her away from all this madness. If he could only sit down with her in a quiet space and talk to her. He desperately needed to tell her he loved her.

"Oh, no," Sophie said with a groan. "This cannot be happening." Her eyes were glued to the descending helicopter.

Noah took his eyes off her and lifted his gaze toward the sky. He studied the helicopter as it lowered for a landing. There was a huge emblem on the side of it. Java Giant.

Java Giant? It was a huge coffee chain. Java Giant was in all fifty states. It was a household name. His employees drank it on a regular basis. He would know that red logo anywhere.

One look at Sophie's face spoke volumes. There was an expression of such dread and angst etched on it. Noah knew that it had something to do with the Java Giant heli-copter.

Suddenly it dawned on him. He hadn't been the only one keeping secrets. Perhaps the person or persons inside the helicopter held the key to Sophie Miller's past.

Sophie stood like a statue as she watched the Java Giant helicopter land on the town green. Leave it to her father to make a grand entrance! Roger Mattson wasn't called "the Entertainer" for nothing. Tall, suave and handsome, with a headful of salt-and-pepper hair, he exuded grace, charm and affability.

As her father stepped out of his helicopter, her first instinct was to rush into his arms and hold on for dear life. It had been over a year since she'd seen him up close and personal. The very sight of him made her want to burst into tears.

She'd never felt so betrayed by anyone as she did by Noah. It felt as if he'd lodged a knife firmly in her back. She'd trusted him! Loved him. Once again she'd been played for a fool.

She felt her knees weakening. Despite everything, she needed her father. It didn't mean that the past had been erased. It just meant she loved him more than words could ever express. And she knew without question he loved her just as fiercely.

Sophie ran to meet him. "Daddy!" she cried.

"Peaches!" he called out, his raised voice textured with emotion. He met her halfway, and they clung to each other as if they were life preservers on the open sea.

The smell of her father's woodsy after-shave rose to her nostrils. She clutched the fabric of his jacket, wanting to hold on to him for dear life. In this moment he was safety, the foundation that would never crumble.

"Don't ever let me go," she whispered, feeling as vulnerable as a child. Being held in her father's arms served as a healing balm. The past no longer mattered in this moment. He had traveled all this way to Love to reunite with her. And she needed him more than ever after Noah's betrayal. She felt as if she'd been stung by a swarm of killer bees. Sophie wasn't sure how she was still standing, when in reality all she wanted to do was fall to her knees.

Noah—strong, hardworking, gentle Noah—had made a fool of her. The man she had fallen in love with didn't exist! Her Noah was a double agent, working undercover for John while romancing her. All she wanted to do right now was melt into her father's arms and get away from all the madness swirling around her. How she felt now was a hundred times worse than when she'd discovered John's duplicity.

Thank you, Lord. For bringing my father back to me just when I needed him the most.

After what seemed like an eternity, her father gently pulled away from the embrace.

His eyes were moist with tears as he studied her face. "Sophie. I can't tell you how good it feels to see you in the flesh."

Sophie felt her lips trembling. "Daddy. You found me." She looked into her father's grass-green eyes. They so closely resembled her own.

A hint of a smile played around his lips. "I've always known you were here in Love, Sophie."

Sophie sputtered. "W-what? And you waited all this time to come and see me?" She supposed it had been foolish of her to believe that a man of her father's vast resources couldn't have located her. Maybe deep down she had known all along he'd had his eye on her. It had allowed her to stand on her own two feet and gain a measure of independence.

"It was difficult, to say the least, but I owed you that much. I knew how badly you'd been hurt. You were so desperate to make a clean break from your life. It's probably one of the most selfless things I've ever done, because I worried about you and almost came here to get you half a dozen times or more. When I was your age I ran off to join the army. My father wanted to stop me, but he realized I had to grow into the man I needed to be."

Roger reached down and caressed her cheek. "You've turned into your own woman, Sophie. One who knows what she wants and the kind of life she wishes to lead. How many ways can I say that I'm sorry, baby girl? I made so many mistakes. I said and did things I deeply regret. And I know how much pain I caused you."

Sophie swiped away tears with the back of her hand. "Oh, Daddy. It was all such a mess. I had no business getting engaged to John. I never loved him. How wrong would it have been to marry a man I didn't love? But I was so wrapped up in making you proud of me. I didn't want to let you down."

"And then I let *you* down," her father said in a tortured voice. "I took John's side when I should have been firmly rooted in your corner. I chose to believe him and his lies, when I know you are the most truthful person I've ever known. As a father, I should have known."

Sophie scowled as John boldly stepped forward. "Sir. I just want to let you know that I intended to tell you about Sophie being here in Love as soon as I straightened things out between us. I'm still very committed to being a part of the family."

Sophie couldn't be certain, but she thought there were beads of sweat on his forehead. Leave it to John to sweat in Alaska!

"Save it, John," Roger roared. "I wouldn't believe a word out of your lying mouth if you had your hand on the Bible. It took me way longer than it should have, but I see your true colors. You were never fit to marry my Sophie. Shame on me for believing you were!"

"Who is this man, Sophie?" Jasper barked, stepping forward so he was standing next to her. His brow was furrowed. "And why did he fly in on the Java Giant helicopter?" A group of residents stood behind him, clearly intrigued by the drama playing out before their very eyes.

Her stomach clenched. Sophie hated the look of confusion radiating from Jasper's eyes. Why hadn't she just told the truth from the beginning? After all this time, what would they think of her? She prayed the townsfolk and her dear friends wouldn't think her whole life here in Love had been a big fat lie.

The crowd around them was growing larger. Sophie felt almost claustrophobic from the way everyone was beginning to press in. Hazel stared at her with wide eyes. For once her dear friend was speechless.

Cameron couldn't seem to look away from the helicopter. Noah stood at the edge of the crowd, taking it all in without saying a word. What could he say? He'd been revealed as a liar and a fraud. And he didn't care for her. It had all been a pretense crafted in order to get close to her for surveillance purposes.

She cleared her throat. "He's my father, Jasper. His name is Roger Mattson. And he owns the Java Giant corporation." Sophie took a deep, fortifying breath. She jabbed a finger in John's chest. "My real name is Sophie Mattson. This man was my fiancé until I discovered he only wanted to marry me because I was Roger Mattson's daughter. If I were to marry him, he knew he'd be in line to inherit the company."

Shocked gasps rang out in the crowd.

"When the bottom fell out of my world, I came here to Love," she explained. "To soothe the pain. To reinvent myself. To get as far away as possible from people who only saw me as a wealthy man's daughter."

"So, you're rich?" someone shouted out.

"You're the Java Giant heiress," Zachariah cried out. "That means you'll inherit the company someday."

Sophie could barely keep her head up. So many pairs of eyes were focused on her like laser beams. "Yes," she said in a shaky voice. "My father is a very wealthy man. But I've always been of the mind that it isn't my money. Not really."

"You knew this town was in bad financial shape, Sophie," Dwight said in a hurt tone. "As town treasurer, I'd like to know if you ever thought of helping us out."

The question hung in the air like a live grenade. Sophie didn't have a single clue as to how to answer it. Part of leaving her life in New York City had meant leaving her big trust fund and bank account behind. And even if she still had access to it, she wasn't sure giving the town a large cash donation would have been the right answer to the long-standing problems. In her opinion, money rarely solved difficulties.

"It wasn't her job to save this town!" Noah shouted from the crowd. The townsfolk parted and he came forward, stopping a few feet away from Sophie. He looked angry and protective, as if he might take on the world on her behalf. Something unfurled in her heart at the sight of him in battle mode. An hour ago it would have made her deliriously happy, but now all it did was make her furious.

"I don't need you to defend me!" she said in a raised voice. She glared at Noah. It hurt to look at him, but she wasn't about to avoid his gaze. His lies hadn't broken her. Even though she loved him and her heart was shattered, she would still hold her head high. He was no better than John, with his secret agendas and lies.

Noah moved even closer. "Sophie, please hear me out. I'd like some time alone with you so I can explain everything," he said, his voice full of tenderness.

It frightened her how badly she wanted to listen to him. How vulnerable she was to his vast array of charms. One word from him and she might just crack and forgive him. But she couldn't. Shouldn't. So many times in the past Sophie had been used as a commodity—by friends, teachers, family members, boyfriends—but she had never imagined Noah would treat her as such. At the moment she felt all used up. She had nothing left to give.

She held her chin up, refusing to budge an inch. She might love Noah, but she was nobody's fool. "There's nothing to talk about. You came here with an agenda, Noah. To spy on me. To profit from doing so. Isn't that right?" Her lips twisted. "You must have laughed yourself silly by how easy it was to fool me into falling for you…sharing my feelings, opening myself up to you, believing in you."

"Everything was real between us, Sophie. You can't fake something like that." Noah had a pleading tone to his voice. "I love you."

The words almost made her knees buckle. A few hours ago those three little words would have sent her soaring into orbit. But now she simply felt numb.

"What are you saying, Sophie? Noah isn't really a cook?" Hazel shouted.

Sophie turned toward her friend. She saw the look of hurt on Hazel's face, and wondered how much of that was due to her. It was embarrassing to air her dirty laundry out here in the open, in front of everyone, but the crowd didn't seem inclined to leave. Matter of fact, some of them seemed to be enjoying it.

"No, he's not, Hazel. Noah is a private investigator hired to keep tabs on me by my ex-fiancé." Her lips quivered. "I was just a means to an end. A big fat paycheck."

The buzzing of the crowd kicked up a

notch. Several residents were openly glaring at Noah, while others were shaking their heads in her direction. Sophie could only imagine their thoughts. People had a tendency to make judgments about a person when they discovered that individual was wealthy. Shyness suddenly turned into snobbery. If you were proud of something it became vanity. Sophie had never wanted to be regarded as anything other than a newcomer to town who worked at the Moose Café.

Ever since her arrival here Sophie had been skirting around the truth, living a lie. She'd told herself that telling a white lie wasn't too bad, but she'd been kidding herself. All to avoid the truth of her real identity and her connection to the Java Giant empire. At first she'd been simply running away from her life and trying to cut ties with her past. Then, slowly but surely, she'd grown to love all the townsfolk, and she had been fearful that they would view her differently if they learned who she really was. As Sophie Miller, she'd been accepted with open arms and as a regular person. Sophie Mattson had always been treated as a commodity, a rich man's daughter.

"Daddy. Please get me out of here," she begged. Sophie buried her face against her father's chest and sobbed her eyes out. He sheltered her in the crook of his arm and led her toward the Java Giant helicopter.

"I've got you, Sophie," he said in a reassuring voice as he settled down beside her in the roomy interior. "We'll be at the Anchorage airport in no time. Then we'll take our private plane back to New York."

All Sophie could do was nod. She was in shock. Pain. Despair. Her heart was broken into little pieces. And she felt so sorry about having misled the people of Love. It was all way too much for her to have to face.

As the helicopter took off, Sophie resisted looking out the window. She knew she must be going crazy, because she thought she heard Noah calling her name above the roar of the blades. She felt her father smoothing back her hair, all the while saying her name in the most tender tone imaginable. It reminded her so much of when she was small and he would comfort her after a skinned knee or a broken toy. She pressed her eyes closed, wishing things could be as simple as when she was a little girl, yet knowing it was impossible.

Noah looked up at the sky, following the progress of the helicopter as it drifted farther and farther away. He placed his hand against his chest as a sharp pain seized him. He knew it wasn't anything physical, although it felt as if he might break in two. He'd lost Sophie, and he had the strangest feeling he might never see her again. Watching her leave with her father was akin to seeing all his hopes and dreams for the future go up in smoke.

Everything he had meant to tell her had been lost in the madness swirling around them. John's appearance. Sophie's devastation. The townsfolk gathered around them. The helicopter coming from out of nowhere.

"Why couldn't you just stick to the assignment?" Noah turned to see Sussex standing behind him. "Now you'll never get your last portion of the money. And you won't get the girl, either." The man made a tutting sound. "Too bad you didn't realize your place, Catalano. People like you don't end up with heiresses like Sophie Mattson."

Noah clenched his fists at his sides. He'd earned the paycheck from Sussex, but at this point, he didn't care about the rest of the money. What mattered most was Sophie. While his mind rejected John's statement, a part of Noah wondered whether Sophie *was* too good for him.

"I've about had it with you," he seethed.

"Why?" John sneered. "Because you don't want to hear the truth?"

Noah took a step toward him, so there was no longer any distance between them. "For being an absolute fool and hurting the woman I love."

Sussex shook his head. "I'm not the only one who caused her pain. But don't worry. I fully intend to help Sophie recover, once I get the opportunity."

Was the man delusional? Did he still truly believe he had a shot with Sophie?

Noah scoffed. "You asked her to marry you for one reason only—the Java Giant empire. Sophie knows it. I know it. And it appears that your boss, Roger Mattson, now realizes it. I'd look for a new job if I were you."

John's face blanched. Noah could see reality crashing over him. With a withering look, he stomped off. Noah could only pray he never saw Sussex again.

Jasper came forward and shook his fist at Noah. "I had a gut feeling you were a snake in the grass. How could you treat Sophie like that?"

"I know you don't like me, Jasper. You've made it abundantly clear. I'm sure you think I'm a low-down dirty dog—" Noah began.

Jasper cut him off, "That pretty much sums it up."

Noah sliced his hand through the air. "I'm not going to argue with you. Trust me, I have more important things to deal with right now. For starters, I have to find the woman I love and make things right. Nothing else matters."

Hazel, with her hands firmly planted on her hips, marched up to him. He braced himself to feel the full impact of her wrath. It gutted him to lose the woman's friendship and respect.

"Is that true? Do you really love Sophie?" she asked in a gruff tone.

"More than my own life." Noah knew he'd never said anything with more conviction. What he felt for Sophie was epic. His throat tightened at the prospect of losing the love of his life.

Cameron walked up and met Noah's gaze head-on. "I consider myself a good judge of character. I don't like the fact that you've been spying on Sophie for her slimy ex, but from what I've seen, you really love that girl. That's got to count for something in this world."

Relief flooded through Noah. At least he still had a few people in Love who believed in him, even though he wasn't certain he deserved the benefit of the doubt.

"So, are you just going to stand here and watch that helicopter fly farther and farther away? Or are you going to fight for Sophie?" Hazel said in a thunderous voice.

Jasper sputtered. "I can't believe you're encouraging this scallywag to try to win Sophie back."

Hazel cut her eyes at him. "Let me tell you something, Jasper. I'm a true romantic at heart. If I wasn't, I wouldn't have waited around for you all this time. How many years did I love you, when you barely knew I was alive? Humph! Way too many to count. People stumble. We all fall at one point or another. We fail to do what's right and we hurt the very people we love the most. I've done it. And so have you. Some of the best couples in this town have had their trials. If I remember correctly, we've encouraged many a couple to fight the good fight. How can we do any less for Noah and Sophie?"

Jasper sighed, then reached out and drew her close to his side. "That right there is the reason I love you to pieces, Hazel Tookes." He pressed a kiss on her cheek. "You're right. If Sophie loves Nickolai here, I'll support it."

"It's Noah!" Hazel, Cameron and Noah all hollered at once. Jasper smirked and ducked his head. Noah knew full well he'd been messing with him all this time. The mayor was as sharp as a tack. He'd known his name from the get-go.

Noah shrugged. "Hazel, I appreciate the support, but I don't even know where to start in order to fix this."

"What we need to do is put our collective thinking caps on. If I know Sophie like I think I do, she wouldn't miss our wedding for anything in this world. She'll be back." Hazel thumped him on the shoulder. "And you need to be ready to lay it all on the line. Do you think you can do that?"

Noah swallowed past the huge lump in his throat. "I don't have a choice," he replied, grateful when Cameron sent him an encouraging nod. "God planted me here in

Love for a reason. And it has everything to do with meeting Sophie and falling in love with her. I'm prepared to do anything I need to in order to win her back. Or fall on my face trying."

Chapter Twelve

Sophie gazed out of the window, silently admiring the view of Central Park from her penthouse apartment. It had been four days since she had left Alaska. Four days during which she had barely eaten or laughed or smiled. Having a broken heart always sounded like such a cliché, but for the first time in her life, Sophie knew how it felt. It made the events of last year seem like child's play. And even though Noah had been the instrument of her pain, she couldn't simply snap her fingers and fall out of love with him.

The distance between New York City and Alaska did nothing to soothe her pain. Being back home didn't mend her heartache. It gave her a buffer against Noah and his lies, but it didn't stop her from loving him. She wasn't sure anything could.

Her father padded down the hall in his robe and slippers. He was carrying a tray of scones and an assortment of coffee drinks. He had a newspaper under his arm. Much to Sophie's surprise, he had taken off a week from Java Giant in order to be with her and help her heal. He poured coffee into two mugs and handed Sophie one. She blew on it, then took a sip, savoring the rich chicory flavor. If nothing else, lying about in her pj's drinking coffee was comforting.

Roger raised his eyebrows at her. "Sophie. You've been moping around for days. There's nothing I want more than to have you here in the city with me, but something tells me your heart and mind are back in Alaska."

Sophie bowed her head. She had cried

more tears in the last few days than in her entire life combined. She'd prayed and cried. Then prayed some more. She lifted her head and met her father's steely gaze. "I don't want to hurt your feelings, but I found a home in Love."

"You didn't hurt my feelings. Parents raise children up to spread their wings and fly. How can I be upset that you found a place to soar?" He narrowed his gaze. "And that young man Noah? What you found with him? It looked pretty serious from where I was standing."

Sophie took a long sip of her coffee. Her father's eyes were probing. "Come on, Sophie. You can tell me."

"I fell in love with him."

Roger let out a sigh. "Finally. I've been waiting for this day for what seems like an eternity."

Sophie let out a hollow-sounding laugh. "I always thought love would lift me up. And it did for a while. But now it's as if someone ripped off my rose-colored glasses and forced me to see reality."

"Reality being that Noah was hired by John to watch you?"

Sophie nodded. "And romance me."

There was a huge lump in her throat. It still felt agonizing to know Noah was so calculating and sneaky.

Her father held up his hand. "I'm not sure I believe that. I saw the way he looked at you, spoke to you. Why would he continue to plead his case after his cover was blown? At that point the jig was up. He wasn't going to gain anything by doing that. And if he was just in it for the money, why was he at odds with John?"

Something flickered inside Sophie as she listened to her father's logical assessment. She so wanted to believe in Noah. Her pulse began to race and she felt a kernel of hope blossoming inside her. She shut her eyes tightly and shook her head. "I'm not going to tie all of my hopes and dreams on a maybe, Daddy. Noah had many opportunities to come clean with me, but he blew it."

"So this adventure in Alaska…is it over?"

Over. The thought of leaving Love permanently was an unsettling one. "I have to go back there tomorrow. Jasper and Hazel are two of my closest friends. They're getting married in a few days and I'm a bridesmaid." For the first time in four days, Sophie grinned. Just the thought of seeing her dear friends tie the knot caused a groundswell of emotion to rise up inside her. She wouldn't miss their special day for anything in this world. "It won't be easy to face everybody, but I'm determined to be strong."

"What about Noah?"

Sophie scoffed. "I'm sure he's left Love by now. After all, he's not really a cook. And there's nothing left for him there now that his assignment is over."

Her father leaned over and placed a kiss on her cheek. "I'll support you no matter what you decide to do. Promise me one thing, Peaches."

"Sure thing."

"Make sure you keep a clear head and an open heart."

Tears misted Sophie's eyes. Her father was being sentimental and so incredibly loving. He had given her a soft place to fall over the past few days. She nodded her head instead of answering. She wasn't certain she could hold it together long enough to reply. At the moment she didn't know up from down. All she knew was that it was going to take a really long time to get over Noah Catalano.

The very next day, Sophie was on her way back to Alaska. After flying to Anchorage, she was met at the airport by O'Rourke Charters. She was now on her way to Love. She peered out of the window of Declan's seaplane and admired the stunning Alaskan landscape. Butterflies soared in her stomach as the beloved fishing village came into view. The craggy mountains and the glistening waters of Kachemak Bay made her eyes moisten with emotion. Sophie placed her face against the glass and smiled as the snow-dusted fir trees came into view.

As they began their descent, she felt her excitement building. It was almost as exciting as the very first time she'd flown into town. This time, too, Declan landed the plane on the water with incredible finesse. Sophie barely felt a thing.

As soon as they disembarked, she asked him for a favor. She needed to see Hazel. "Declan, I need a ride to the Black Bear Cabins. Can you swing me over there?"

He flashed her a brilliant smile. "Anything for you, Sophie. It's sure good to see you back where you belong. And right in time for the wedding tomorrow."

Sophie grinned at him. In spite of everything, it felt good to be here. She had no idea if she was back in town for keeps or simply sticking around long enough to be a part of Jasper and Hazel's wedding. How could she remain in Love when there would be so many memories of Noah everywhere she looked? Wouldn't it be better to go back to New York City and work on her relationship with her father?

Declan dropped her at the main lodge, sending her off with a wave and a promise to see her at the wedding. Sophie walked up the steps toward Hazel's front door. She stood on the porch for a few minutes, suddenly feeling awkward. What if Hazel rejected her? What if she was angry Sophie hadn't told the whole truth about her origins?

No! Sophie knew her friend better than that. She was the most accepting woman in the world. If anyone would have her back it would be Hazel. Sophie rapped insistently on the door. Although Hazel had an open-door policy, Sophie knew her appearance might be a surprise.

When the door swung open, Hazel greeted

her with a loud shriek. She wrapped her up in a gigantic bear hug and almost squeezed the life out of her. Then she tugged on her coat sleeve. "Come on inside. You had me scared you might miss my wedding, although my gut told me you never would."

"I'm sorry I left so abruptly. Everything happened all at once. I barely knew if I was coming or going," Sophie explained.

"Oh, pish tosh!" Hazel said with a dismissive wave of her hand. "You don't have to explain a single thing to me, although I would have loved knowing about your connection to Java Giant. The Moose Café could have benefited from a few pointers." Hazel winked at her. "And now I know why you took to being a barista so quickly. You were a ringer!"

Sophie let out a sigh of relief. "I came here looking for a fresh start. I should have told you my real name ages ago. Forgive me, Hazel."

"There's nothing to forgive." Her friend reached out and gently shook her.

"Thanks for saying so." Sophie felt as if a huge weight had been lifted off her shoulders.

"You won't believe what happened while you were gone!" Hazel's voice sounded almost like a shriek.

"At this point I'll believe anything," Sophie said, her own voice dripping with sarcasm.

"Guess who came back to Love day before yesterday?" Hazel didn't wait for her to answer. "Marta! She came back with a story about a sick relative and a reading of a will." Hazel rolled her eyes. "Long story short— she asked for her job back at the Moose Café. And Cameron agreed, since Noah—" Hazel stopped talking midsentence. She clapped a hand over her mouth. "Sorry to bring up his name, Soph."

Sophie tried to shake it off as if it didn't bother her. "No worries. I'm glad the Moose

Café has a cook now. I hated the idea of leaving you high and dry with the waitressing."

"We understood your predicament. Honor and Grace came in to cover some shifts. We made do." Hazel locked eyes with her. "Have you spoken to Noah at all? I noticed you haven't been answering your cell phone."

"No. I haven't. I can't." Her hair tumbled about her shoulders as she fiercely shook her head. "I came back for the wedding. Nothing else."

Hazel clapped her hands together. "Speaking of the wedding, I've got lots to do before tomorrow morning. I could use a bridesmaid's help."

"Whatever you need, I'm at your service," Sophie said, bowing to Hazel as if she were royalty.

"Let's get to it, then," she exclaimed. "I've got my final gown fitting and I need to check in with Gracie and make sure Jasper got the marriage license." She threw up her hands. "It will be a wonder if I get it all done."

Sophie spent the remainder of the day helping Hazel with the final wedding details. As she made her way all over town, she was met with support and love. Not a single person denounced her for keeping her heritage a secret. One local wanted to know if a Java Giant would be opening in Love. Sophie had been happy to tell her it wasn't going to happen. Cameron had worked hard to build up the Moose Café. He certainly didn't need a huge corporation to come in and steal his thunder.

At Hazel's request, Sophie stayed over with her at the lodge. Early the next morning all the bridesmaids convened at Hazel's house. Not one of them peppered Sophie with questions about Noah or her unexpected exit from town. Nor did they ask her a single thing about being the heiress to the Java Giant fortune. It made Sophie realize that she might just have the very best friends in the world.

When it was time, they drove with Hazel to the church, where they helped her get dressed in her beautiful gown. They complimented her and took pictures with their phones and cameras. Hazel said she had never felt so lovely.

As the wedding march played, Hazel walked down the aisle with as much elegance as a queen. She looked stunning in her blush-colored gown. Sophie walked behind her with the rest of the bridesmaids. The church was filled to the rafters with townsfolk. It was a virtual sea of people—sitting, standing, pouring out of the church. Sophie couldn't believe her eyes when she spotted Dwight holding hands with Marta and looking deliriously happy.

Jasper stood at the altar with his groomsmen beside him, looking as proud as a peacock. His chest was puffed out and the smile etched on his wizened face was gigantic.

He stepped forward to meet Hazel. Tears fell from his eyes as he said, "Thank you for joining me on this journey, my love."

Pastor Jack began the wedding ceremony by inviting Hazel and Jasper to step forward to the altar. Sophie sat raptly and listened to every word, every nuance. It felt as if love was vibrating from every corner and pew of the church.

"You may now recite your own vows," Pastor Jack announced, nodding at Jasper to begin.

Jasper reached into his pocket and took out a handkerchief. He dabbed at his eyes. "Hazel. I've given you a lot of guff over the years. It took me way too long to recognize you as my life partner and not just as my best friend. You are an exceptional woman. Generous. Loving. And probably the kindest woman I've ever known. I'm not sure if a grumpy old man like me deserves a woman as fine as you, but I'm determined to spend the rest of my life making sure you know the depths of my love for you."

Hazel reached out and smoothed her hand across Jasper's cheek. "My sweet Jasper. Even when you're grumpy and out of sorts, I always know that your heart is as wide as Kachemak Bay. There isn't anything you wouldn't do for the people you love. You're loyal and loving and true blue. And I can't imagine loving anyone more than I love you."

At Pastor Jack's urging, they exchanged rings. "I now pronounce you husband and wife," the pastor announced with a flourish. "You may kiss your lovely bride, Jasper."

As she watched the bride and groom exchange a tender kiss, tears ran down Sophie's face and she felt as if her heart had swelled to ten times its original size. There was so much love inside this church that it threatened to reduce her to a puddle of tears. This couple was living proof of the existence of love and the glory of God.

When she began walking down the aisle behind the bride and groom and the rest of the bridal party, she realized she'd left her bouquet in the pew. Once she retrieved it, she turned to head back down the aisle. Noah was standing in front of her, almost as if he had materialized from thin air.

Sophie let out a low moan. She wanted to pivot around and run in the other direction, but she didn't want to give him the satisfaction of knowing he'd rattled her. She wanted to display a small measure of dignity. He'd broken her heart, but she was still standing.

"Sophie." The raw edge in Noah's voice made her shiver. He sounded like she felt. In pain. A little bit broken.

"I—I have to go," she whispered, tearing her eyes away from the sight of him. In his dark suit and tie, he looked spiffy and way too handsome for his own good. She made an attempt to get past him, but he reached out and tenderly grasped her wrist, lightly enough that she could have easily released herself.

"Please don't go. I need to talk to you."

She shook her head. "There's nothing more to say. None of it was real. Don't you think I know that?"

"I love you. That's as real as it gets. When I accepted the job, you were nothing but a name on a piece of paper. I took the assignment out of sheer desperation." He winced. "My security company in Seattle is having financial problems and this was my big opportunity to rescue it and keep my employees on the payroll. I should have seen the warning signs with John, but I didn't. In the beginning I thought you were the person he made you out to be—cold, calculating and disloyal. But during my time here in Love I got to know you, Sophie, and I realized you were the real deal."

Sophie began to cry. She put her hands up to her face and sobbed. She wanted to believe Noah so badly, but with a past littered with people who'd used and betrayed her, she wasn't sure she could. She couldn't stand the idea of being hurt again by Noah.

"I don't know what to believe," she cried.

She felt Noah's hands prying her hands away from her face. Sophie looked into his blue eyes and saw love shining in them. "Sophie. All I cared about before I came to Love was getting the money to stabilize my company. Before John showed up in Love I was prepared to tell you the whole truth, because when it came right down to it, you trump everything else in my world."

Sophie blinked at him. "You were?"

Noah nodded. "Yes. When I began to fall in love with you I knew that huge lie might destroy everything for us. Even though I was afraid, I was prepared to tell you the truth. Sophie, you're the most important thing in my world. Nothing else even comes close."

"Noah!" Sophie said, her voice full of emotion. She buried her face against his chest. He rocked her back and forth, all the while crooning words of reassurance and love. She pulled away from him, meeting his gaze head-on. "You do love me. I can see it in your eyes. And I can hear it in your voice."

"Yes, Sophie, I do love you. Very much." He reached out and wiped away her tears with his finger. "I came to this town as a cynic." Noah scoffed. "I took the assignment because I saw a little bit of myself in Sussex. A man who got jerked around by his ex. And I seriously needed a big paycheck."

"You're nothing like him!" Sophie said.

"No, I'm not. But at the time I believed he was wronged in the same way I was deceived by Kara. Sophie, from the very first moment I met you I should have seen the truth shining right back at me from your beautiful eyes. I got in over my head. And the moment we began a relationship I should have told you the truth. All of it."

Sophie nodded. "Yes. You should have."

"I was too afraid of losing you. So I hesitated. I'm so sorry that you didn't hear the truth from my lips. But there's one truth only I can tell you."

"And what's that?" she asked. She knew in her heart Noah was her match, the one she'd been searching for all this time. Her heart hadn't betrayed her. And neither had Noah.

"That I love you. I am hopelessly and hopefully in love with you. I'm hoping that you'll forgive me, because you're the best person I've ever known. And I want to show you how much I adore you, Sophie. Not just in one grand gesture, but in a hundred different ways over weeks and months and years. I want to be yours forever if you'll let me."

"I do forgive you, Noah. You're human. You made a mistake. I know you well enough to know you're not hateful or vengeful. You wanted to make things right by telling me the truth. I know how much that might have cost you with your company."

"Strangely enough, Sussex paid me in full. The money showed up in my account yesterday. I think he was afraid I might take him to court." Noah chuckled.

"That's wonderful," Sophie said.

"I don't care if you're the cobbler's daughter or whether your father is the president of the United States. None of that matters to me in the slightest. I love you for you. Because you greet each day with a sunny attitude and a smile. Because you try to lift everyone up when they've fallen down. And you have the cutest freckles I've ever seen. I love you, Sophie, despite your odd taste in grilled cheese sandwiches and the fact that you have a lead foot."

"I do not!" Sophie objected. "I'm a very reasonable driver."

Noah reached out and took her hands in his. His moves were tentative, as if he wasn't quite certain whether or not she would reject him. "Please know that I'll always tell you the truth. From this moment forward."

"I believe you, Noah. I know your heart. And I love you very much." She wiped tears away from her cheeks. "The people of Love have forgiven me for not telling them about being the Java Giant heiress, so I guess we're both forgiven," she said with a grin. "We both have a clean slate here in Love."

"Chalk up another success story for Operation Love," Noah drawled.

"I thought you weren't in the Operation Love program," Sophie teased.

"I am now! You made a believer out of me, Sophie Miller." He laughed. "I mean, Sophie Mattson."

Noah dipped his head and placed a triumphant kiss on Sophie's lips. The future was stretched out before them—a glorious beacon of love and light and endless possibilities. And it would all unfold in Love, Alaska—right where God had planted them.

Epilogue

"Mmm. I think that I like this one the best," Noah said as he took another sip of the frothy mochaccino. He was sitting at a table at the Moose Café with Sophie, tasting various coffee drinks she'd whipped up for him. She'd turned him into a coffee lover ever since the Taste of Love event. Now that Marta had come back to Love, Noah was putting in only a few hours here and there until she got back into the groove in the kitchen. He was working remotely for Catalano Security and spending as much time as he could with Sophie between her shifts.

Hazel walked over to the table and placed a mug in front of Sophie. "Here's a little concoction I've been working on. I'd be mighty pleased if you gave it a try." She winked at Noah, who pretended not to see her none-too-subtle gesture.

"That's so sweet of you, Hazel," Sophie said, gently lifting the mug and taking a sip. She began to sputter, and quickly put the drink back down. "It's a little bitter," she said, wiping her mouth with a napkin.

"Why don't you give it a swirl with the spoon and maybe it will taste better," Hazel suggested, pushing the cup back toward Sophie. Noah let out a quiet groan. Things weren't exactly proceeding according to plan. Hazel was overplaying her hand.

Suddenly Jasper appeared at Hazel's side and began tugging her by the arm. "Come on, woman. Give the lovebirds a little privacy."

Sophie cocked her head to the side as Hazel and Jasper walked away, bent together as they whispered back and forth. "Is it me, or were they acting strangely?"

"To be honest, they're always a little odd," Noah said with a shrug. "Nothing more than the usual."

Sophie giggled and lightly swatted his arm. "That's not nice."

"I mean it in a totally good way, of course," he added. "Those two are incredible. Matter of fact, everyone in Love is pretty fantastic. I've been welcomed like I was born and bred here. It makes me feel like I'm back in my hometown."

Sophie's grin was infectious. "Me, too. Being in Love reminds me so much of Saskell and all of the wonderful things I experienced there. I think what it boils down to is that we feel at home here. And there aren't many places in the world that feel like home."

"Now that you mention it, I think home is a feeling." He reached out and took her hand in his. "You make me feel at home, Sophie.

When I'm with you, I know I'll never need anything more than the two of us to be completely over-the-moon happy."

"Oh, Noah. I feel the same way. I've always dreamed of being loved by someone who sees me as I am and loves me just the same."

He leaned over and placed a tender kiss on her lips. "Who wouldn't love you, Sophie? You make it effortless."

Sophie let out a contented sigh. "We sure owe this town a debt of gratitude. If it wasn't for Operation Love and Jasper's extraordinary vision, we might never have ended up together. And God made sure we were both planted right here in Love so we could find each other."

Noah held her face between his palms and looked deeply into her emerald eyes. "I would have found you, Sophie. If I had to look in all of the fifty states, I would have tracked you down. My heart would have led me straight to you."

"Call me crazy, but I believe it," Sophie said, sniffling back tears. "You make me feel as if anything is possible."

Noah pushed the coffee cup toward her. "You're sure you don't want to give this another try?"

Sophie scrunched up her nose. "I didn't want to hurt Hazel's feelings, but it's pretty awful. It tastes like mud."

"This was supposed to be a little more seamless," Noah muttered. He let out a sigh. "Sophie. Look at the spoon."

She gazed down at it, then shrugged. "What? It's just an ordinary spoon. It looks pretty old, now that you mention it."

"Really look at it, sweetheart," Noah said in a coaxing tone.

Sophie pulled the spoon out of the cup and gasped. "There's something written on it."

"It's a Catalano family heirloom," Noah explained.

Sophie reached for her napkin and wiped off the liquid residue. She blinked a few times, then swung her gaze up to Noah. "'Will you…marry me?'" she asked, reading the words engraved on the spoon.

Noah locked gazes with her. His heart began thumping wildly in his chest. There was so much riding on this moment, so many things he wanted to say to this woman he loved so dearly. "I love you, Sophie. I've told you that a hundred times or more. But more importantly, I hope that I've shown you my love and devotion. I came to this town in a bid to save my company. At the time it seemed as if it was the most important thing in my world. It didn't take me very long to discover I was wrong. You, Sophie, you are my world. Nothing is more important to me than you. And the scariest feeling I've ever known is when I thought I'd lost you.

"I never want to feel that sense of loss. Not ever again. Because you're a keeper, Sophie Mattson." He stood up from his chair, then promptly got down on one knee. The sound of Hazel squealing in the background rang in his ears. He knew that dozens of people were gawking at him from their tables, but he didn't care one bit. If he could, he would shout his proposal from the rooftops of Love. He no longer had a single thing to hide.

Noah reached into his pocket and pulled out a ring with a yellow string tied around the band. He looked up at Sophie, who was staring at him with a shocked expression etched on her face.

"Sophie, I want to be your husband. I want to show you for the rest of your life that I appreciate you for who you are and not for your father's riches. Honestly, I couldn't care less about that. From the moment I first laid eyes on you I felt a pull in your direction. You just kept tugging at my heartstrings even though I tried my best to ignore it."

He let out a shaky laugh. "In the end, I tumbled right over the edge in love with you. And I know with a deep certainty that I'm going to love you for the rest of my days.

Will you marry me? Will you say yes to a lifetime of loving each other?"

Sophie was now openly sobbing and wiping tears from her face. In one hand she was clutching the sterling silver spoon. Before he knew it, she had wrapped her arms around his neck and was hugging and kissing him.

When she finally let him go, Noah asked, "Is that a yes? Because it sure seems like one."

"Of course it's a yes," Sophie said, tugging him to a standing position. She rose on tiptoe and placed a resounding kiss on his lips. The sound of wild clapping rang out in the Moose Café, along with shouts of congratulations. Right on cue, Noah reached for her ring finger and slid the diamond solitaire onto it.

"I want you to know that I asked your father for his blessing." Noah smiled tenderly at Sophie. "And he gave it to me wholeheartedly."

Sophie appeared to choke back tears. "That means the world to me."

"I thought this ring was perfect for you. I knew it had to be beautiful just like you, but more importantly, I knew you wouldn't want anything flashy or over-the-top. So I picked something that sparkled like the sun, because that's what you do, Sophie."

She looked down at the ring on her finger. The smile on her face let Noah know in no uncertain terms that he'd made the right choice. "It's gorgeous. Just perfect. I almost want to pinch myself to make sure I'm not dreaming."

"You're not dreaming. Pretty soon we'll be walking down the aisle and picking out a house to live in. A wonderful life is waiting for us. Right here in Love. I can run Catalano Security remotely from here in town and travel back to Seattle when necessary."

Jasper approached Noah and clapped him heartily on the back. "I'm sorry if I gave you a hard time, Noah. But your fiancée is near and dear to my heart." Tears pooled in his eyes. "I'll have you know that I consider Sophie to be an honorary granddaughter. I'm mighty happy the two of you found each other. Not that you need it, but you have my full blessing."

"I appreciate that," Noah said, clasping Jasper's hand. "Sophie thinks the world of you."

"She's been like a ray of sunshine in this town. She has a knack for making everyone feel happier for having been in contact with her. No one knows how to turn a frown upside down like Sophie," Jasper declared.

"That's my girl," Noah said, reaching out to Sophie and pulling her close to his side.

"I am your girl, Noah. Now and forever," she promised, then planted a tender kiss on his lips.

Afterward, Noah sheltered her in the crook of his arm. "I can't believe how blessed we are," Sophie whispered, looking up at her fiancé with love shimmering in her eyes.

As Noah glanced around at all the people who were supporting their engagement and future marriage, he knew with a deep certainty that their union would be blessed by their families and the entire community of Love. He pulled Sophie even closer. "With love, everything is possible," he told her, knowing in his heart that they would always be surrounded with an abundance of love.

* * * * *

If you enjoyed
HIS SECRET ALASKAN HEIRESS,
look for the other books
in the ALASKAN GROOMS *series:*

AN ALASKAN WEDDING
ALASKAN REUNION
A MATCH MADE IN ALASKA
REUNITED AT CHRISTMAS

Dear Reader,

Thank you for joining me on this Alaskan adventure. I hope you enjoyed Sophie and Noah's love story. I really enjoyed writing *His Secret Alaskan Heiress*, particularly since Sophie has always been one of my favorite characters. I really wanted her to find her happily-ever-after. The town of Love, Alaska, serves as the perfect backdrop for falling in love. Snowy tundra. Moose crossings. Reindeer pizza. The Moose Café! There's so much to love in this wonderful town.

Sophie and Noah are both suffering from the same ailment. Both characters have been betrayed in the past by someone close to them. As a result, they are both wary of falling in love. They both have scars that need to heal. And thankfully, they find joy and a happy ending in each other's arms. Noah and Sophie find a warm community in the small fishing village. The town of Love provides Sophie with a loving, supportive home where she is accepted for reasons unrelated to her bank balance. Likewise, Noah finds a warmth and acceptance in Love that reminds him of his hometown and the family values he grew up with. In the end, forgiveness is a big theme in the story and Sophie, in particular, needs to forgive Noah and her father in order to move forward with her life.

I feel very fortunate to be writing for the Love Inspired line. Being an author is my dream job. I enjoy hearing from readers, however you choose to contact me. You can reach me at scalhoune@gmail.com, at my Author Belle Calhoune Facebook page or at my website, bellecalhoune.com. If you're on Twitter, reach out to me, @BelleCalhoune.

Belle Calhoune

OCT 2017